Big Bay
Fate Under the Golden Gate

Reggie Brick

Reggie Brick Books

Contents

Dedication IX

1. Late Night Chase 1

2. Juggling Men 15

3. Big Decisions 25

4. Horsing Around 41

5. Cable Cars and Sea Lions 49

6. Luck 63

7. Route 66 71

8. Arrival 81

9. Cloudy Skies 89

10. Mount Tam 103

11. Streets of San Francisco 113

12. Hippy Dippy 123

13. Making it Nice   133

14. Making of a Bad Guy   141

15. Fade to Black   149

16. New Digs and Santa Cruz   159

17. Moving Day   169

18. Big Gestures   183

19. Kiwi Hospitality   189

20. Agriculture and Alps   201

21. Last Night and Flight   213

22. What Ifs   223

23. Rumblings   233

24. Outside Looking In   243

25. Reconsideration and Magic   253

26. Angel and Demons   261

27. Crazy Daze   271

28. Shifty Treats   279

29. Kiwi Magic   287

30. Birth Days   297

Also by Reggie Brick   307

Dedicated to . . .

My loving husband who inspired the best parts of Neve;
and to
family and friends
who have supported me along the way.

Chapter 1

Late Night Chase

At night, the darkened hallways at the hospital always gave Jenae pause because hardly anybody was around except for the second nurse on the other side of the ward—and the nursing assistant who was busy tending to his patients. Working a normal daytime schedule was Jenae's ongoing fantasy and the reason she ultimately wanted to work in administration. She knew that the goal would be met as long as she stuck with the plan and paid her dues. Jenae churned away at making her dreams come true by studying for her MBA during the week and working twelve-hour shifts at the big medical center in downtown Dallas on the weekends. Night shift was all that was available to her when she returned from Hawaii on her three-month traveling nurse stint over the summer. Her nurse manager fulfilled the promise of hiring her back, but Jenae wasn't thrilled about struggling with the night schedule. Pay was better than day shift, nevertheless, acclimating to sleeping during daylight hours was a challenge. Gremlin, her terrier dog, loved having her mistress home most of the week because it meant hanging out in the shade by the pool and getting lots of pats from the other residents of the apartment complex. While Gremlin socialized, Jenae double tasked tanning and sleeping with a towel over her face.

As Jenae made 4 AM rounds on her patients, Saturday night turned into Sunday morning. She caught a glimpse of a shadow that passed by the nurse's station at the end of the hallway. *Hmm, that's odd; maybe it's a lab tech coming for a timed specimen, or a resident looking for a snack.* She softly knocked on her last patient's closed door and peered inside before she quietly entered, closing the door behind her. Jenae washed her hands in the sink and even gave her dolphin heart bracelet a scrub with soap and water before drying them and approaching the bedside table. Her patient was sound asleep while Jenae checked his wristband, hung a piggyback antibiotic to his IV bag, and assessed his bandage sites with the help of a small flashlight that she pulled from her fanny pack. She counted his respirations as the attached monitoring equipment spit out his latest blood pressure and heart rate readings. After documenting the patient data on her report sheet, she pushed the door open a few inches by backing up into it and bumping it open with her butt; she scanned the room one final time, then peered out into the hallway to see a man hunched over an electronic box with an antenna sticking out. She gasped and jumped back into the room, startled by the stranger lurking in the shadows.

The stranger moved back and forth as he walked down the hallway; like he was scanning the beach for lost diamond rings. He turned a knob on his electronic box and stopped at an isolation cart outside of a patient's room. He turned his back from where Jenae was observing and opened the drawers to pull out a disposable gown, hat, and mask. When Jenae peeked through a slit in the door, she saw him almost completely covered, which concealed his identity except for his piercing green eyes. She caught a glimpse of the side of his face when he bent down to put on booties. He opened the patient's room door across the hall and glanced around, looking for something or someone. As he fully entered the room, Jenae tiptoed to the treatment room close by and softly locked the door. She observed him from a small window with metal mini-blinds as the hair on her neck stood up. He emerged with narrowed eyes and quickly moved closer to the treatment room guided by the screen on the tracker. He stopped with a jolt when JT, the rather large and imposing nursing assistant, approached him with a bundle of soiled sheets in his arms.

"Can I help you?" JT asked in a deep, bellowing voice.

"Uh, no. I'm just here for my uncle. He's a patient on this floor."

"Visitors aren't allowed until 11 AM. You certainly shouldn't be wandering the halls in the middle of the night. What's his name?" JT was annoyed and wanted him off the floor as soon as possible.

"It's um . . . David Smith."

The nurse assistant checked his roster. "I don't see a patient named David Smith on this floor. Perhaps you can check with the operator to find out if he is still a patient here and visit when the sun comes up. But for now, you need to leave." JT's angry voice sent a very clear message. He was tired and knew this guy was up to no good.

"OK, sorry sir, I'll do that."

"And take off that isolation gear. It's for hospital employees and known visitors only. You look ridiculous." *Dumbass.*

The green-eyed bandit removed the gown and mask, threw it in the trash and nodded with a salute to the linebacker-sized nurse assistant before walking toward the elevator bank. Jenae waited several minutes to calm down, taking deep slow breathes before she exited the locked treatment room and hurried to the nurses' station. She grabbed her patient charts and moved to the medicine room to log her notes and medications for the shift. Her fingers trembled as she punched the code 43321 to enter the room and threw the charts on a tall countertop. As Jenae pulled a screeching stool forward to sit down, she looked out over the nursing station through a one-way glass window and saw the green-eyed bandit turn around. Without hesitation, he walked back from the elevator bank, clearly holding the electronic device under his folded coat. He looked behind him and leaned his body sideways to peer down each hallway before he grinned, looked up, and approached the medicine room. Holding her breath, Jenae hopped back and ducked under the countertop when he approached and cupped his hands around his eyes, inches from the window. "Ah ha!" the intruder uttered as he identified what he wanted in the room. He rounded the corner after checking that both ways were clear and grabbed the handle of the door to the medicine room. It didn't open; he muttered to himself as he shook it back and forth, as if he could force it open with his strength. Jenae squeaked a tiny peep and unhooked the phone receiver from the wall and pressed '0' for the operator.

"Hello, this is Jenae on 2 West T. We have a code black. Please send security to the nurses' station, STAT."

Instantly a woman's voice boomed over the intercom, "Code Black to 2 West T nurses' station. Code Black to 2 West T nurses' station." JT, the nurse assistant, opened the door of a patient's room to hear the intercom more clearly and jogged to where Jenae was holed up in the medicine room. The green-eyed bandit ran for the stairwell when he saw JT and the security officers emerge from the main corridor. He only had two flights of stairs to run before hitting the exit door and disappearing into the bushes at dawn's first light. Scary situations were commonplace in the hospital, but they usually involved compressing a patient's chest to keep them alive; or keeping a mentally ill patient from assaulting the staff. Remaining calm was paramount for patient care, but that didn't mean that Jenae didn't drive home with tears running down her face at least once a month. It was time for another emotional release.

"What was that all about?" JT asked Jenae as security rushed down the exit stairs to look for the suspicious stranger.

"I have no idea. It did seem like he was looking for me, though. I was ready to jab him with a 60 cc syringe of potassium chloride if he broke into the room. I think he was using a tracker, but what is he tracking? I don't recognize that guy." Jenae's hands stopped shaking as she inspected her stethoscope and rifled through her fanny pack looking for a bug. She pulled her shoes off and looked at the rubber soles for any signs of tampering, nothing.

"What about that bracelet you have on? Could something be in one of those charms?" JT asked.

"I doubt it. My so-called long-distance boyfriend, Neve, gave it to me when I left Hawaii a few months ago. He's still in New Zealand."

"Maybe that creep was looking for drugs."

"That's probably it. He really wanted in the medicine room; he's just some freak trying to get a fix."

After handing off patients to the next shift, JT hung around to walk Jenae to her car in the parking garage. They rode the elevator to the first floor of the hospital. Before reaching the garage elevator bank, Kristine an old roommate grabbed Jenae's arm to ask about the Code Black that was called on her unit.

"You can go on JT. I don't want to hold you up anymore. I'll be fine," Jenae said.

"Are you sure? I don't want you to be scared of this guy," JT responded.

"I'm positive. I'll walk out with Kristine. You've been great. Go ahead and get back to your family—I bet they're already dressed for church."

"See you next week, then. Don't study too hard!"

"Bye JT. Thanks for saving me!"

Kristine and Jenae sat down at a wobbly table at the hospital lobby coffee shop after ordering drinks and breakfast. Kristine folded up a napkin and placed it under the short leg to stabilize it.

"It's weird how I can go straight to sleep after drinking a fully caffeinated mocha," Jenae said.

"You're right, that's weird—I can only have chamomile tea before bedtime. Maybe you're overtired. Do you want some of my quiche?"

"No, I'm allergic to eggs, remember? I'll just stick with the coffee."

"Oh yeah, I forgot about the egg thing. So, what happened with the guy running out of the hospital? I heard he was trying to break into the medicine room," Kristine asked.

"It's a good thing JT was there. I felt like the guy was coming after me. I hid in the medicine room. But after thinking about it, he probably was just trying to score some morphine or codeine," Jenae said.

Kristine's ears perked up and her head tilted like a puppy when she heard bells chiming from the church across the street from the hospital.

"Hey, do you want to come to church with me before heading home? I usually go after my shift on Sunday morning. It's the Catholic Church, so we can show up in our scrubs. They don't care how you're dressed," Kristine asked.

"Gosh, I haven't been to a Catholic Mass since I wore a fluffy sea foam long gown in my nursing school friend's wedding. She married a doctor by the way. Sure, let's go. I have some favors to ask of the Big Guy."

The worn-out nurses looked both ways before quickstepping across a four-lane boulevard to join other parishioners walking into the stain glassed entryway. The 8 AM service was crowded, and the nurse pair found two seats in a dark corner at the end of pew. "There must be an early Cowboys game today . . . so many people here," Kristine said. Jenae nodded as she looked over the sanctuary. Halfway through the service, Jenae found she was sleeping instead of praying for forgiveness as she kneeled with her forehead resting against her folded hands. Parishioners stood up around her in a line to go to the front of the church; she leaned back on the pew to let them pass because she wasn't Catholic and knew she couldn't take their Eucharist. As she looked down the empty pew, she blinked her eyes and rubbed them because she thought she saw the green-eyed bandit standing in the doorway, scanning the church. *No, I'm probably just dreaming this.* His gaze moved in Jenae's direction, and she lifted her jacket around her head as she slipped out of her pew and ducked behind the line of people on the side of the sanctuary. Her heart jumped in her chest in fear. *Shit, it's him, the green-eyed bandit. Sorry, Lord.* Jenae looked down at her coveted bracelet that Neve gave to her from Hawaii, unhooked the clasp and reluctantly stuffed it behind a statue of Mary. She lowered her head and slipped out of a side door before Kristine could return to the pew.

⸺◆⸺

Gremlin bounced and barked when Jenae returned home from work, and they immediately skipped down four flights of stairs to the open field next to the apartment complex to do doggy business. When Jenae worked long twelve-hour shifts (which usually turned into fourteen hours with the commute), her neighbor across the breezeway let Gremlin out throughout the day using the front door key left under the mat. After a dozen throws of the tennis ball, Gremlin huffed from exhaustion and laid down. "Come on, girl, let's grab the mail before we go inside." Gremlin followed her to the mailbox station in the middle of the apartment parking lot and Jenae pulled out a wad of letters from her locked box. "Bill, bill, bill. I hope there's a letter from Neve. Oh, here's a letter from Maribelle from Australia. Remember her, Gremlin? She stayed with us for a month in San Antonio in that little apartment. She was on that Rotary trip for student nurses. OK, I could use this, a coupon for an oil change. Oh weird, and another letter from Australia; this one is from Adelaide too, but it has different writing." Jenae dug her finger under the flap at the top and ripped the envelope open. She unfolded the paper and looked at the signature first. "It's from Marvin. He was a Royal Australian Air Force officer that I met in Hawaii this summer. Let's see, he's back to normal duties in Adelaide and is basically saying that he misses his vacation in Hawaii with his blokes and can't find anyone to date in Adelaide." Gremlin gave Jenae a lick to the face when she sat down on the curb to finish the letter. Jenae scratched Gremmie's belly as the dog rolled around in the cool grass. "Let's see what Maribelle has been up to." Jenae put the bills and coupon in her back pocket and opened the other Australian post. "Oh, no. She's broken up with her fiancé recently and is having a really hard time. I bet she is. She's been with that guy for years—I think he was her first love." Jenae picked up her opened letters and put them side-by-side. "Maybe Marvin and Maribelle need to meet, Gremlin; they could go out on a date together. I am going to send them each other's addresses and they can figure it out from there. We're matchmakers, Gremlin!" Jenae patted the dogs head and Gremlin gave her owner an open mouth doggie smile.

Jenae filled Gremlin's bowls; one with kibble and a few bites of sausage and the other with fresh ice water. Then she checked and double-checked the locks on the door and windows before she closed the blinds. She checked the answering machine, which had a message from work wanting to get more information on the incident, and one from Kristine, wondering why Jenae disappeared from church, and if she was all right.

While she finished her bowl of oatmeal with blueberries and Diet Coke, Jenae returned the call to hospital security. They told her that cameras had captured the identity of the green-eyed perpetrator at the hospital, and he was a known sexual stalker by the Dallas Police Department. They felt confident that he would be picked up and put back in jail soon. Jenae told them about her tracker theory and the bracelet that she left behind in the church. They were skeptical but would send a security officer over to retrieve it and check the bracelet for any tracking devices.

"Just keep your head on a swivel and lock your doors at all times. We will contact you when he is apprehended. You should probably stay away from work until then."

"I'm not scheduled again until Friday, but I'll do as you say. Thanks, officer." Jenae fell asleep until early afternoon.

When she awoke, Jenae remembered that she hadn't returned Kristine's call and left a message on Kristine's answering machine. "Hey it's Jenae, I'm OK. I thought I saw that creeper again at the church, so I took off and I'm safe at home now. Thanks for checking on me. Call me later." The one person Jenae really wanted to talk to was Neve. It had been a month since she had received a letter from him. They'd been writing faithfully for the first few months apart, but the letters from New Zealand had dried up. They didn't call each on the telephone because long distance charges were prohibitively expensive, but Jenae was willing to take the hit one time to get a feeling of support and security from Neve.

Buurt, burrt. The phone rang in Jenae's ear.

"Hello?" Neve answered in a drowsy voice.

"Hi, Neve? It's Jenae." Her voice cracked, and she sniffled.

"Jenae! Is everything OK? Why are you crying?"

"I haven't gotten any letters from you for a month, and I had a really bad night at work. Why haven't you written to me?"

"I'm sorry. I've just been busy at work with my brother, and we've been busting our arses on our flip house late into the night. I really want to get it finished and sold so that I have a nice nest egg when I come to America again. My cousin said that I could still live with her family for a while until I get a place of my own."

"I'm sorry that I'm crying, but I was worried that you'd changed your mind. And I had another weirdo following me at the hospital last night."

"You've got to be careful, Jenae. You're too nice to people."

"Well, I don't think it's that. I can fill you in on the details in a letter when I find out more about this guy."

"I'm coming to San Francisco, Jenae. I really am coming in a few months, and I can't wait to see you again. Why don't you move to the Bay Area? Your brother's there, you can finish your MBA at one of the colleges there, and you can find a nursing job easily."

"Maybe I'll look into it more seriously. But I'm not coming until you're already set up there."

"I'd love it if you did. And I promise to write to you tonight, no matter how late it gets after painting the house."

"I better let you go, or I'll have to work another shift at the hospital to pay for this phone call. I can't wait for your letter. Big Kiss." Jenae touched her lips and blew a kiss to the air.

"Big Kisses. Bye, bye."

Chapter 2

Juggling Men

J enae was told Calculus 501 in business school wasn't as difficult or as rigorous as the regular kind taught in the hard sciences, but she felt like the math problems were forging painful new pathways through the white matter of her brain. She spent half the day on Saturdays in tutoring class just to pass the exams with a B so that she could continue with her MBA studies. On the first day of the semester, a petite, blonde, sporty professor addressed the class in a big auditorium. She announced, "you are in the gatekeeper class, calculus; if you don't receive an overall C or above, you will be removed from the MBA program. Look around, after the first exam 25% of your classmates will be gone. After the second exam, another 25% will drop because they cannot make a C for the class. If you are in the 50% still here to take the final exam, feel proud of yourself to walk out of here with a B. Very few students will receive an A in this class." Jenae's competitive spirit engaged; she looked around the room and thought, *Yep, I can beat out at least fifty percent of the people in this room. But I better get some help immediately.*

Tutoring class monitored by three Middle-Eastern, male, grad students, including one slightly built Israeli, one large boisterous, Turk and one quiet Iranian, became an enjoyable part of her week. She learned enough about writing proofs and how to use her expensive HP calculator to get her through to the 600 level classes of business school, and she made good friends and laughed a lot in the process. Her tutors were surprised that she showed up every single week, and they became fast friends. At the end of every tutoring session, the Turk announced, "OK, everyone. Pull out a fresh piece of paper. We are going to do one final proof; at the top of your paper, write *The Meaning of Life.* And nobody gets to go home until you've solved this problem." The big Turk laughed and laughed until tears formed in his kind brown eyes.

The ratio of men to women in the MBA program strongly favored the men as they were mostly there because their companies paid for advanced studies. Jenae used her beginner's enthusiasm to join study groups and create new friendships. Kyle and his single Texas A&M buddies were in her marketing and microeconomic classes. They lived in a shared house and all of them worked at engineering firms in Dallas. They were thrilled to have Jenae in their social circle because she brought cute young nurses to their house parties that often turned into shades of frat bashes.

Jenae flirted with her TA in her computer skills course to try to get an "A" out of the class that she struggled with and despised. The TA was reasonably cute and extremely tall at 6-foot 6-inches. He gave her lots of attention. After class one evening, they walked to the parking lot together.

"I get the feeling that there is something between us. I would like to ask you out, but I can't while you are still my student. Maybe we can do something together after finals."

"Sure, maybe. We'll have to see how it goes. Do you run?" Jenae asked.

"I like to run on the golf course at night when it cools down and the sprinklers are watering the grounds."

"OK, I'll keep that in mind," Jenae teased.

Jenae always held Neve in her heart, but she wasn't sure if it would ever work out between them, with him still living in New Zealand. He had said and done the right things, but logistically, it seemed impossible, and her intuition told her that something was off. Kyle and his A&M buddies didn't boost her confidence, either.

"Ah come on, Jenae. Why are you messing with this guy from New Zealand? What's wrong with us American dudes?"

"All y'all are OK, but I'm swinging for the fences. He is much better looking than any of you cowboys, and he has a sexy accent." Jenae smirked.

"We have Texas accents and are a lot more fun. And we live in the United States of America."

"The world is my oyster, Kyle. I'm going for broke. I'm taking the bull by the horns, big risks get big rewards; however you want to say it. I'm going to go for the gusto while I can."

"Alright, alright. This guy must be really great. I can't wait to meet him. He'd better live up to the hype."

A letter arrived from Neve a week and a half after Jenae's conversation with him on the phone. The envelope was thin with a red and blue border with the word "POST" marked on the left corner. The stamp with the picture of a kiwi bird foraging in a forest was canceled with squiggly black lines. When she saw his handwriting, she took in a deep breath of ease; it was similar to the comfort he made her feel in vulnerable situations.

The letter from Neve was two thin pages long and was written on both sides in blue ink. She settled in on her couch with Gremlin at her feet to read it. Neve told Jenae all about his house flipping project and that he and his brother were going to list it on the market in the next few weeks after the final touches to the kitchen were made and the landscaping was installed. Since he was a real estate agent, and his brother was a broker, they didn't have to pay realtor fees and they had the inside track to potential buyers.

Neve told her about meeting an Air Force pilot and crew from Seattle who flew frequent missions to Antarctica. He met Deely at a local bar in the hotel where the flyboys stayed before heading south. U.S. pilots were sometimes stuck in Christchurch for a week or more before the weather would allow flights into McMurdo Station on Ross Island. The winds and frigid temperatures were difficult to predict, and the past month had been especially brutal for Deely's crew. Neve and his brother stopped at the hotel bar most nights after working at their nearby flip house, and they struck up a weeklong friendship with the Air Force crew. Neve got excited thinking about flying . . . big or little planes; he just wanted to get into the cockpit. He had dreamed of becoming a pilot since he was a young boy watching airplanes from his back garden. Deely convinced him to take a flying lesson before heading to America and gave him his number in Seattle if he needed any advice once he got stateside.

Neve told Jenae in the letter that he was ready and willing, while he was still young, to go out into the world and lose everything if it meant pursuing his dreams . . . and she was a big part of his dreams. In the last paragraph of the letter, Neve casually mentioned that a girl that he had dated off and on before his Hawaii trip had shown up on his doorstep last month. She'd been having some health issues, and he helped her out. The ex-girlfriend was persistent in trying to start their relationship again, but Neve said no. He was definitely going back to America, and their relationship was finished once and for all. The XOXO at the end of the letter didn't land favorably on Jenae's heart, especially since this was the first that she had heard of the ex-girlfriend. She questioned what Neve's true intentions were. She cared deeply for him, but thought, *does he have true feelings for me?* She wanted to keep her options open in case the entire relationship was a mirage in her mind.

Jenae pulled out pictures from her summer in Honolulu and placed them in small photo books that held one photo per side. She had them developed when she first returned to Dallas, but hadn't taken the time to sort through them and throw out the fuzzy, out-of-frame shots. She always got double prints to share with her friends. Past pictures of memories were fun inserts for birthday cards and thank you notes. Sometimes her mind played tricks on her and she wondered if she even remembered what Neve looked like because it had been a few months since they had seen each other. She worried that she wouldn't be attracted to him when she saw him again. But when Jenae found the photos of Neve and her together on the beach, her heart thumped a little bit harder, and she couldn't shake the butterflies in her stomach. She remembered the sensual heat she felt when she was next to him and the fun they had playing on the beach and in the bedroom. He was really hot, too; perfect muscles, washboard abs, and the face of a movie star. After holding the pictures to her heart as she lay back on her pillow, she slowly snapped out of her love trance and grabbed another envelope and flipped through more photos. "Oh, look, Gremmie, here is a picture of Johnny from Boston." Gremlin was a willing listener as long as someone was scratching her belly. "I went out with Johnny in Hawaii, too. He's really smart, but he is too stuffy for me. He's cuter than I remember."

The very next day after class, Jenae heard a message on her answering machine, "Hi Jenae, this is Johnny. I hope you remember me from Hawaii. It's been a few months, but it took me this long to track your number down. Listen, I'm coming to Dallas next week for a work trip and was wondering if I could take you out for a margarita and some Tex-Mex food that you were telling me about." Jenae paused and rewound the machine to listen again. The message made her heart feel warm and giddy; she felt wanted. Even though it was 11 PM on the East Coast, she called the number back. "Hi Johnny, sure I will join you for dinner when you're in town. I'll have to work around my school and work schedule, but we can figure it out."

⎯⎯◆⎯⎯

Jenae pulled into the front circular entryway of a four-star hotel in downtown Dallas. When she walked around the car to the front lobby, she saw Johnny in a starched white shirt and suit pants talking to the concierge. He had a big smile on his face when he spotted her and almost skipped to give her a big hug.

"Mm, its so good to see you again, you look great!" Johnny pushed her back by her shoulders, as he looked her up and down.

"Thanks, you look good too, in your professional garb. It's a bit different from the board shorts in Hawaii," Jenae replied.

"I took the tie and jacket off for a more casual look. We all have to grow up some time, I suppose."

The hostess at the trendy Mexican restaurant sat the pair at a patio table on the terrace. A warm balmy breeze and the nightlights of downtown Dallas was the perfect backdrop for Jenae's lime margarita on the rocks with a half-salted rim. Johnny toasted with his bottle of Corona, "cheers, to meeting a beautiful lady in beautiful places."

"You're so sweet. How's the horse broker business in Boston treating you?" Jenae asked.

"The industry is so specific and I'm on a steep learning curve right now, but I get to travel a lot, and Dallas is one of the places where we have clients, so hopefully I can see more of you when I'm here," Johnny said.

"Sure, that'd be great," Jenae, said.

"Are you dating anyone seriously? I've thought about you a lot since I've been back on the East Coast."

"I go out with different people. I don't have a ring on my finger yet. Besides, between school and work, I really don't have the time to devote to a relationship," Jenae said.

Jenae had no trouble compartmentalizing her love interests. She still went on dinner dates with men who were more interested in her than she was in them. The self-instigated date-to-dine program gave her socialization with stimulating conversation while replenishing leftovers in her refrigerator.

The secret to keeping it casual was to date men who lived in different cities and limit her affection to a hug and a quick kiss at the end of the night. Her goal of getting married and creating her own family started with figuring out which man would be a great father and provider. But more importantly, she needed to figure out which man made her whole body want for more. She wanted to find that one special man to love for the rest of her life.

Chapter 3

Big Decisions

The uncertainty of uprooting her life and starting over in another big city like Neve had asked was overwhelming for Jenae. It came down to the stick and the carrot. Neve was a pretty big carrot and moving to a hip big city was exciting to think about, but really scary, too. The stick was Jenae's tiring of the Dallas single life. She'd gotten the most out of dating and partying, and Jenae was ready to settle down with the right guy. She loved Dallas, and felt she made the right move when she relocated there from San Antonio because it made her grow. Dallas was bigger, shinier, and more glamorous, with greater opportunities. She loved San Antonio when she moved from Kansas straight out of nursing school because of its vibrant culture, and when she settled in, she found the people were down to earth and good.

Another stick was the uncertainties about the predator from the hospital. Jenae felt better about the incident, especially after security called to tell her that the green-eyed bandit had been picked up by the cops and was sitting in jail awaiting a hearing, but the justice system wasn't fool proof. He was being held for sexual assault charges and the police were looking for more victims.

Dallas was where her roots had been planted for a few years, but she seriously thought of moving to San Francisco to join her insta-love hunk, Neve, whom she had met on a beach in Hawaii. *What am I thinking? It's crazy to just change schools and jobs and states. And what am I going to do with Gremlin? Will I find an apartment in San Francisco that will let me keep her? And what happens if Neve and I don't work out? I could stay with my brother until I find a place to stay. The green-eyed bandit could be released from jail, and he could start stalking me again if I stay here.* Her heart was full and shredding at the same time. She had an excellent relationship with the staff at her hospital. They were supportive of her travel nurse summer in Honolulu and her pursuit of her MBA and even suggested that they could help her move up in administration. She had fun loyal friend groups and DFW was an excellent airport for travel when she got sick of them. She prayed that the answer would come to her in a definitive way.

Jenae grew up with siblings who easily flung themselves to different states and to faraway parts of the world. It was natural and normal for them to evacuate Kansas for a bigger frontier. Living in the heartland in the same home all childhood, gave them the roots and stability they needed to venture out on their own. Although they were scattered around the world,

Jenae's six siblings always returned home for the holidays with their parents—in big, traditional family style.

◄O►

Neve unpacked his three suitcases on a queen-sized bed of his cousin's guest room. He was exhausted from the sixteen-hour flight to San Francisco with a layover in Honolulu, but the tropical stop reminded him of the best two weeks of his life. He was excited to be in America to make a go of it, and anxious to see if Jenae really would join him in San Francisco.

Neve's cousin was married, and their two young children spent most of their time in the backyard pool. The pool, along with a massive outdoor kitchen area, filled the entirety of their backyard at their home in the East Bay. Their family life was a good example of what Neve could have in his future. His cousin married an American and adjusted from her New Zealand culture, worked at a tech company and was very content. However, even though they shared the English language that was essentially the same, customs and innuendos were an adjustment, and missing her family was a constant stressor.

The plan was for Neve to stay with his cousin until Neve's brother, Hamish, arrived and they would set up an apartment, buy a car, and find some kind of work. They were willing to work construction under the table until a work visa came through. Neve's attraction to Jenae was augmented by the possibility of marrying an American to live in the States permanently. He couldn't be 100% sure about Jenae or living long term in a foreign land until he had spent "real life" time there. His six-month visa would be long enough to figure that out.

The second day on American soil, Neve called Jenae. His knees felt weak as the phone rang at her apartment, brrring . . . brrring.

"Hello?" Jenae asked as she picked up the phone.

"I made it to San Francisco. This is Neve."

Jenae squealed with elation. "I can't believe you're here! How was your flight?"

"It was long, but good. I got to stretch my legs in Honolulu when I changed planes and it's still hot there. The pilots out of Honolulu let me come into the cockpit while we were flying over the Pacific. I wish I could have ridden up there the whole flight," Neve said.

"That was nice of them. What are your plans? When can I see you?" Jenae replied.

"I heard there are cheap flights to Dallas on Southwest Airlines. Can I come to visit you there early next week?" Neve asked.

"Sure! You can stay as long as you want; I'll show you around." Jenae could hardly contain her joy; she wanted to run out on the balcony and scream.

"I can't wait to see you; we don't have to write letters to communicate anymore. I can just call you. What a relief," Neve said, as his stomach churned from enthusiasm.

"I have bad news, though. I had to ditch the cute bracelet that you gave me from Hawaii," Jenae said.

"What bracelet?" Neve asked.

"You know, the one that you put in my backpack. I found it with the card that you wrote me. You know, on the plane ride back from Hawaii," Jenae said, confused.

"That bracelet wasn't from me," Neve responded, just as confused.

"But it was two dolphin charms with a heart in between them. It's so cute, you don't remember? It reminded me of us playing in the ocean. It was with your note," Jenae explained

"You must be confused. Who else could have put that in your bag?" Neve was annoyed.

"Shit. Maybe that guy at the hospital was trying to get to me after all. I felt like he was tracking me, and he lost me after I tossed the bracelet," Jenae surmised.

"But you got it in Hawaii? Oh, I wonder if the FBI agent that was stalking you is behind this. I knew he was a psychopath," Neve added.

"The guy at the hospital was not Logan; he was some troubled green-eyed guy off the street."

"Yeah, but I'm sure Logan has lots of people that owe him favors. Have the police checked the bracelet for a bug?"

"I'll call them later and ask them about it. Now I want you to come here sooner, so that you can be my big, strong protector," Jenae said with a high-pitched flirty voice.

"I'll keep the bad guys away, but you won't be able to protect yourself from my desire for you," Neve said, to match his cheesy smile.

Her breath quickened as she lengthened her neck. She imagined what being in Neve's arms would feel like again after months apart. Thoughts of a soft kiss, the smell of his skin, and melting her body into his was overwhelming. She felt excited and grateful as her skin tingled. "OK, it's settled. I need you here right now," Jenae said, and let out a deep sigh.

"You know I'd be there in a flash if I could. Let me check into flights," Neve said as he grabbed the yellow pages and opened it to the airline section.

<hr>

Jenae stood at the back of the airport gate seating area as she scanned every face that walked off the jet way at Love Field. The flight from Oakland made two stops on the way to Dallas in what was routinely called the milk run flight, but the price was right.

Neve grinned at Jenae, and his blue eyes sparkled with relief when he caught her gaze. He was exactly as she remembered him in Hawaii. Neve dropped his bags and leaned into her arms and wrapped her in his embrace. They gently mumbled sweet nothings as they buried their heads in each other's necks. After the initial energy surge was released, they sighed and smiled and grabbed hands. Jenae led them to a private corner of the airport terminal. They locked eyes and Neve placed both hands on Jenae's jawline; his gaze moved to her moist lips, and he gave her a slow, passionate kiss. Jenae swooned as she closed her eyes, arched her back; and with a stroke of his tongue, she melted into his warm, delirious universe. They didn't notice travelers taking second looks as suitcases noisily rolled past them, nor did they care.

Neve loved dogs, and when they arrived at Jenae's apartment, Gremlin greeted him by jumping up and down, then licking him on the face as he sat on the couch in a fit of laughter.

"I guess you're a good guy, after all. Gremlin has given her approval. I'd say that was a magical feat, but Gremlin loves everybody."

"She is really cute for a small terrier dog. I've only had big dogs—a German shepherd and a yellow Lab. They were introverted compared to this little one." Neve scratched Gremmie's neck, and she rolled onto her back for a full belly rub.

"Let me show you around. We're in my living slash dining room. I mostly study on my kitchen table here, and through there is my tiny kitchen with the pass-through counter. Do you want something to drink? I have a pitcher of iced tea and orange juice."

Jenae poured two glasses of unsweetened tea over ice, and handed one to Neve.

"It works because I don't cook much for just myself, but I do host some small potluck dinners for my friends," Jenae said.

"I can only boil vegetables, but I did bring you a Christmas fruit cake all the way from my mom's kitchen in New Zealand," Neve said.

"Is this a joke? Nobody eats fruitcake. I thought it just got passed around like a white elephant gift," Jenae said.

"Not in New Zealand. I love homemade fruitcake. Feel how heavy it is. There are tons of dried fruit and nuts in there." Neve pulled the plastic wrapped brick out of his backpack and handed it to Jenae.

"Wow, who knew? The only fruitcake I've tried was on a dare. I did try Vegemite from my Australian girlfriend, Maribelle. She lived with me in San Antonio for a little while on an exchange program."

"Did you have it for breakfast? Did you like it?"

"Not really. It tastes like B vitamins in a jam."

"That's basically what it is. Vegemite on toast is a great hangover remedy. I'm not really a fan either, but the Aussies love it because they were raised on it from a young age, I suppose."

Jenae grabbed Neve's hand and walked him through the doorway into the bedroom.

"Wow, you have a king-sized bed! I've never had a king-sized bed. Only in America."

"There's lots of room and if anybody asks, we make a pillow barrier between us. There is definitely no spooning going on," Jenae said, half kidding.

"Got it. But that's just when the lights are on, right?" Neve asked.

"I have a lot of nosey friends and I like to keep them in the dark as much as possible," Jenae asserted.

Jenae had finished her classes for the week and called in sick from work at the hospital for the entire weekend and wasn't on the schedule for seven more days. After sixteen hours of private sexy time that included two trips to Blockbuster for new VHS movies with Neve, Jenae loaded up the trunk of her Toyota Camry with a picnic basket, an old blanket, and Gremlin. As they drove out of the parking lot, Gremlin pushed her way onto Neve's lap and stuck her wiry-haired face into the wind. She panted with a doggy smile and barked at fellow canines walking on the sidewalk with their owners.

"Have you ever seen the TV series Dallas?" Jenae asked Neve.

"I might have seen an episode when Karl and I were traveling in the States. We don't have that show in New Zealand."

"See that big white ranch house with black shutters way over there? That's Southfork Ranch. It's the main home base for the series and the opening shot of the show. The main characters are J.R. Ewing, Bobby and Pamela Barnes.

They wear big ten-gallon cowboy hats. J.R. is played by Larry Hagman; he also played the astronaut, Major Nelson, in 'I Dream of Jeannie.'" "We will have to watch it together. It's a dramatic nighttime soap opera."

"Oh yeah, I know 'I Dream of Jeannie.' I loved watching it on TV after school when I was a kid. Mostly, I liked Jeannie's skimpy outfits and wanted to be a pilot."

"She was a sexy genie, and Major Nelson played a great straight man for her antics."

Storm clouds built over the ranches of northeast Texas on their way to their picnic spot at Lake Lavon. Jenae kept driving in that direction until Neve spoke up.

"Jenae, I think we are going to drive straight into that wall of water ahead of us. Maybe we should pick a drier spot for lunch."

"I wanted to take Gremlin to the lake, but yeah, you're right. I bet those clouds have hail in them, too. Look, they're turning greenish-gray. That's a sure sign that a tornado's about to pop out."

"I've never seen storm clouds this big. Nothing like this can develop over our islands," Neve said.

"I'm used to them growing up in Kansas."

Jenae took a U-turn on the county road and drove south to her old neck of the woods in Central Dallas. She'd lived in a rental house near White Rock Lake with two of her nurse friends; she was closest to Kristine because they worked at the same medical center. The three of them often threw house parties in their 1940s rental home with a big front terrace and private backyard. They each had different friend groups, so when they all came together for a beer bash, the party often got too big, and the friendly police usually showed up and wished they could join in. Jenae always invited the members of her Master's swim club. Kristine was friendly with resident doctors and beer salesmen, and the third roommate invited fire fighters and hip music groupies. More than once, Jenae's heirloom jewelry went missing after a big party.

"OK, so this is the house that Kristine and I lived in a few years ago. See that shed in the back? The landlord was illegally renting it out; he didn't cause any problems, but it was still weird that the guy was cooking dinner on his hotplate twenty feet from where I slept."

"You need to be more careful!" Neve said.

"That's not the creepiest part. Even though the owner was married and in his late thirties, he kind of wanted to hang out with us. He seemed like a nice guy but asked to come to our parties. We told him 'no' of course, but toward the end of our lease, he came to our front door and asked if we would get any 'extra' narcotics from the hospital for him. He was a total coke head," Jenae said.

Gremlin sniffed the air as the Camry rounded the streets circling White Rock Lake. Wispy clouds blew by in the stiff breeze, but they had escaped big storms from the north. The Dallas Botanical Garden was a jewel property on the lake, with its manicured walkways and grand sculptures. Jenae had passed by the garden every week on her 12-speed bike with her buddies from business school. The bike gang made it a social event even though the guys competed hard to go the fastest, which often left Jenae lagging behind with a red face and puffing hard to keep up.

"Here's a sheltered spot close to the lake. It's not too windy here." Neve shook out an extra-large king-sized comforter onto the soft green grass and placed rocks on each corner to keep the breeze from lifting it up. Jenae placed the picnic basket in the center to cover up one of the torn spots on the well-used blanket. Jenae and Neve walked Gremlin on her leash along the shoreline as they pointed out the different kinds of birds floating in the distance. Gremlin sniffed and pissed along the way and was careful not to get her feet wet above her ankles. Tiny ripples on the surface of the lake sometimes turned into mini white caps. Neve bent down and picked up a few flat rocks near the waterline.

"I used to love skipping stones when I was a kid. My parents would take all of us kids to the river on Sundays for a picnic like this." Neve bent over sideways and flung the rock parallel to the water's surface.

"Count how many times it skips . . . one, two, three, and four. Now it is your turn, Jenae."

"I've never done this before. In my neighborhood, we used to throw stones across the creek in a playful rock war with our friends, but never with any finesse. In fact, I think my brother chipped our neighbor's front tooth in a battle between the sexes."

Neve stood behind her and placed a smooth stone into her hand.

"Hopefully your aim is straight out to the middle of the lake, so we don't need any emergency visits to the dentist. Now, hold it with just your thumb and your first two fingers. Swing back and keep the stone even with the ground, release when your hand is straight ahead. Now, the most important part . . . Give me a kiss for good luck." Jenae smiled and gave him a sweet kiss on the lips. She thought through the instructions as she swayed her arm back and forth three times. The stone was released as a crow cawed from a large tree above; it skipped just once before it submerged to the muddy bottom in the purlieu of newly hatched tadpoles.

"I'm giving the kiss all the credit for that one skip. Let's go unpack that basket. Is there anything to eat besides red wine and fruit cake?" Neve asked.

The skies began to develop into storm clouds above the lake as Neve, Jenae, and Gremlin finished the goodies in the basket. As they buckled into the Camry, Jenae pointed toward downtown.

"My work isn't too far from here. Do you want to see the med center?" Jenae asked.

"Sure, I'm up for whatever you want to show me."

"There are lots of buildings all connected, but I work in that one on the second floor." Jenae pointed to the labyrinth of pristine white structures of the medical center.

"Is that where you were when the creepy guy came after you?"

"Yep, he didn't have far to go to reach the fire escape door. And across the street is the church where I was when he popped his head in there."

"That's where you ditched the bracelet? Did they ever recover it and check it for a bug?"

"I called and left a message with hospital security but haven't heard back about that."

"Do you remember where you left it? Maybe we should go look for it in case they haven't found it. The church looks open."

"How about if you go look for it? I feel kind of weird, besides someone needs to stay in the car with Gremlin. I shoved it behind the Mary statue on the left side of the church."

"Ok, circle around the block and I'll meet you out front." Neve hopped out of the front passenger seat as big drops of rain started to hit the sidewalk in front of him. He ran in through the front door of the hollow church and stopped in awe to look around and take in the beauty. Neve enjoyed the familiarity of the Catholic Church. He had been raised in it as a boy, and his family attended regularly together until his parents divorced. He spotted the Mary statue as he saw a young priest walking toward him. Neve looked at Jesus above the Altar, crossed himself, looked down, folded his hands, and inconspicuously moved to a pew next to Mary. When the priest disappeared through a side door, Neve felt around in the small space between the wall and the statue, pulled the charm bracelet out, and shoved it into his front pocket. Jenae negotiated the corner of the city block and Neve ran through heavy rain to quickly jump back into the front seat of her car.

"That was fast. Did you have any luck, or was the building locked up?"

"Got it." Neve dangled the bracelet in front of the steering wheel. "Let's get back to your place to see if anything is in the charm."

"Oh my God, I'm scared to find out," Jenae scream-whispered as she looked around to make sure nobody saw them.

Chapter 4
Horsing Around

The pair were content with each other in very ordinary situations. Jenae was encouraged that Neve felt comfortable with her lifestyle and that he loved Gremlin, too. But the true test was if he was compatible with her very judgmental friends. There wasn't much time to get showered and dressed for a planned dinner out with her MBA buddies. Jenae had agreed to pick up Kristine at her new apartment near the steak and seafood restaurant on Greenville Avenue. Kristine had recently broken her arm in a car accident and broken off her relationship with the boyfriend who rolled her car with her in it.

"I can't get into these charms with your butter knife," Neve hollered.

"Maybe we can try after we get back from dinner and the rodeo tonight. We're running late, and the storm isn't going to help us to be on time."

Red taillights, bright white head beams, and heavy rain made Central Expressway an extra-long and challenging commute. The MBA bros laughed while taking shots and toasting beer glasses at the bar. When Neve and Jenae arrived at the restaurant with Kristine, the MBA bros stopped and stared.

"Well, well, well. If it isn't Neve, the perfect man from down under. It's good to meet you, man." Kyle shook his hand and the other bros followed suit.

Neve felt intimidated, but didn't flinch on the outside. "Yeah, it's nice to meet you blokes. Jenae has told me a lot about her studies. Sounds like a lot of hard work to me."

"Guys, I brought my friend Kristine along. I don't think you've met, but Kristine and I work together, and we were roommates in a house downtown."

Kyle's eyes lit up as he awkwardly shook her non-casted hand.

Dinner started with an appetizer of New Zealand green-lipped mussels and ended with steaks and more cocktails. Neve told stories about living in New Zealand and retold off-color sheep jokes. Kyle drank way too many shots and gave Neve a seal of approval in between back slaps and saying, "I love you, man."

Jenae looked at her watch and said, "Hey guys, thanks for meeting us for dinner, but we need to skedaddle because I got tickets to the rodeo, and I think it already started."

"Boo Hiss!" Kyle responded.

"Also, I was wondering if one of you sober guys could drive Kristine back to her place, because she rode with us."

"Yea! Of course, sweet Kristine can hang with us."

"Be careful Kristine, I usually can vouch for these guys, but call a cab if they start acting too weird." Jenae and Neve headed out of the restaurant for Neve's first rodeo.

Their seats were on the second row of the metal bleachers close to the bullpen. They made it in time to watch the last rider in the bucking bronco competition, but were amazed by the bull riders and the fact that rodeo clowns distracted the angry bulls long enough for riders to escape the arena through metal guard fencing. One rider wasn't so lucky and was carried out unconscious on a stretcher with an ambulance waiting in the wings.

Young boys about seven years old laid on the backs of sheep, holding onto the wool under the neck while the animals ran full speed across the soft dirt arena. It was all worth it for the finishers, who won cash prizes by holding on for dear life. The top prize went to little José with a time of 39 seconds. The border collie controlling the herd startled little José's sheep, and he got bucked off instead of having the cowboys gently lift him off like the others. Next up were teenage girl barrel riders; some were rodeo queens with tiaras mounted on their cowboy hats. They showed speed and agility as they raced their horses through the obstacle course of barrels. The crowd cheered on the riders as they circled barrels and were loudest on their final sprint to the finish line.

A cowboy entertainer entered the arena on top of a shiny turquoise pickup truck. He wore white pants and a red fringe shirt as he performed elaborate lasso spinning and roping demonstrations. He finished on the dirt in the middle of the arena with exploding flaming lassos.

A final round of bull riding finished out the competition with the winner wearing red-fringed chaps.

"Wow, it's just like in the movies. They are real life cowboys showing off their ranch life talents. I am not as tough as those guys, no way. I've never even ridden a horse," Neve said.

"What? But I thought New Zealand was mostly ranch and farmland."

"It is, especially on the South Island, but mostly farmland with sheep. My future brother-in-law, Bill, is a sheep farmer, and he gets around on a four-wheeler while his border collies run alongside. He controls them with special whistles and voice commands."

"I'd love to see border collies on a working farm; to watch them split a herd up and move them into paddocks. I hear they're the smartest dogs out there. Gremlin wouldn't know what to do with a sheep."

While waiting in a muddy traffic jam to exit the parking lot, Jenae was anxious to bring up the ex-girlfriend that Neve had mentioned in a letter.

"So, who is this ex that showed up to see you last month?" Jenae asked.

"I should have told you about her sooner, but in my mind, it was really over and I didn't want to worry you or complicate our situation."

"Were you still seeing her when you came to America — when we met in Hawaii?"

"Well, kind of, but not really. We'd put things on hold and agreed to see other people. I went on vacation and gained perspective, and while I was there, I decided that it was not going to work out between us, full stop."

"You said she was sick. Is she OK now?" Jenae asked.

"She needed a procedure, and I offered to give her some money for it. She's fine now."

"What kind of procedure? Don't you have national healthcare in New Zealand?"

"We do, but it doesn't pay for everything. She got into trouble with a guy while I was gone. She got pregnant."

"So, you paid for her abortion?" Jenae's voice raised an octave.

"Listen, I know what you're thinking. I wasn't the father, OK? I'm certain of that. She came to me in a desperate situation because the guy she'd been with was a real jerk and she was afraid of what he would do to her. I talked to her about her decision and helped out a little bit financially."

Jenae fell silent and clenched her jaw as she steadily navigated the dark, muddy road ahead. She didn't know how she should feel. She'd taken care of dozens of premature babies and abortion wasn't in her psyche. She understood how a woman could feel trapped by an unwanted pregnancy, but she also worked with a lot of moms who gave their babies up for adoption to couples yearning for their own child. Nothing seemed fair.

By the next morning, Jenae had forgiven Neve for the ex-girlfriend. A good night's sleep made her feel clear minded. She felt like she was Neve's girlfriend now, even though they hadn't discussed exclusivity because they'd been on opposite sides of the world. She also decided that she would officially end her communication with Boston Johnny.

They spent the entire morning lying in bed reading the Sunday paper, eating Christmas cake, and drinking hot tea. Neve inspected the bracelet one more time and determined that he couldn't get into the charms without crushing what was inside, if there was anything at all.

"That's ok. I'll take them into the detective, who is pushing to get this guy as much jail time as possible. Maybe they'll have a way of uncovering something."

"I'll feel better when it isn't in your possession anymore, just in case there is a tracker," Neve said.

"You know, maybe it doesn't have anything to do with that FBI guy. I dated a guy before you last summer. Maybe Tim left it in there when he dropped me off at the airport to come home."

"Who the hell is Tim? It sounds like you are throwing this in my face. Are you mad at me because an old girlfriend came sniffing around?"

"Maybe a little mad. I dated Tim before I met you in Honolulu. He turned out to be a scumbag, but yeah, you're right. And for the record, I haven't talked to Tim since I left Hawaii, and don't have plans to anytime soon."

The drive to the airport was quiet, but hopeful. Jenae had agreed to visit Neve in San Francisco once her finals were over. He was going to focus on finding a job and a place to live in the meantime. They parked the car in a wide-open short-term parking lot and walked into the terminal building, holding hands with their fingers intertwined. Until Neve's flight was called, they stood arm in arm, laughing, kissing, and hugging. Jenae got teary-eyed as he turned to wave goodbye to him at the jetway, but she had so much to look forward to in the future. She couldn't wait to see him in San Francisco in a couple of weeks.

Chapter 5

Cable Cars and Sea Lions

Finals left Jenae's GPA in good standing, but she was mad that the tall awkward TA gave her a 'B' in his basic computer class, even after all of that flirting. *Hell to the no, I'm not going running with that guy anytime soon,* Jenae thought as she packed her bags for her trip to see Neve in San Francisco. JT, the nurse's assistant at work, agreed to take Gremlin for the week. He and his wife had met Gremlin at a party and offered because they lived on a farm outside of town and knew that their kids would love her. They'd been begging for a dog for months, and this was a good opportunity to test one out.

⸺◆⸺

Jenae's brother left his old silver Alpha Romeo convertible, in the parking garage at the San Francisco Airport with the key underneath the floor mat on the driver's side. He had called Jenae from the airport to let her know where he'd parked it, and that he'd left a hand-drawn map to his house in the glove compartment. Her brother lived in a nice rental home in the hills above Palo Alto, and his roommates were Stanford graduates who worked at a start-up company called Apple Computer. They were gracious hosts and allowed Jenae to take over their main living room as her guest bedroom for the week. She didn't hang out much at the house with her brother gone, which made going out with Neve and seeing the sights much easier. Across the Dumbarton Bridge to the East Bay with the convertible soft-top down, Jenae sportily drove to see Neve in the East Bay. Her brother had half-jokingly warned her not to wear a long scarf in his car because a famous actress had accidentally killed herself while driving across the Golden Gate Bridge. She broke her neck or was strangled when her scarf caught in the back wheel of her convertible.

Neve's excitement swelled as he watched Jenae pull up to the front curb. She caught his eye through a dining room window, where he'd been drawing comic book characters with his artistically gifted second cousin. The sunshine was warm and bright as Neve walked to the tiny sports car to greet her.

"I like your style. What are you doing in this neck of the woods?"

"I heard there was a hot young Kiwi staying here. Do you want to go for a spin?" Jenae said.

"Sure, but first come inside and meet my cousins."

Neve opened her door and when she stood up; he gave her a big hug and squeeze before he kissed her lips modestly because he knew prying eyes were watching from inside the house.

"I'm so glad you are here. I've missed you."

"Me too. I have been thinking a lot about us. I mean you."

Neve's cousin invited them in for a cup of tea and biscuits (cookies) and a quick chat. She was kind, and Jenae could tell that she was protective of Neve. He was a good influence on her children; she was grateful to have him around because her husband traveled a lot for work.

"I think we're going to take off now. Jenae has her brother's car, and we are going to the city to check things out," Neve told his cousin.

"Have fun. Neve, you have a key to get back in, yeah?"

"Sure do, thanks. We might be out past your bedtime."

The drive to the city was a blur as Neve and Jenae talked and joked the whole way. Their route took them up the East Bay, through Oakland, across the Bay Bridge in a thick fog past Yerba Buena Island, and into the Embarcadero. They parked at the wharf where it was sunny again; only the bay was covered in a thick, soupy fog. Echoing foghorns blew from ships invisible from shore. The starry-eyed couple found a vendor on Pier 39 selling clam chowder soup in sourdough bread bowls. It tasted creamy and salty and quintessentially San Francisco as they sat on a bench overlooking the boat harbor. When Neve got to the end of his soup, he tore off pieces of his bowl and threw them to the seagulls and pelicans below. Sailboats were tied up to the berths beneath, and sea lions barked and jumped up on the boardwalk to bask in the sun. It was fun for tourists to watch, but a hazard for the sailors tied up at the docks.

Boaters perilously navigated through the maze of threatening and toothy, sunbathing sea lions to try to get back to their vessels.

After lunch, the lovebirds made their way to the cable car turnaround spot nearby. Although some riders were local commuters, most were tourists who wanted to experience old time technology.

"Rice-A-Roni, a San Francisco Treat," Jenae sang the jingle when she saw an advertisement for the boxed rice on the side of the cable car.

"Never heard of it," Neve responded as they jumped onto the car and hung on to shiny brass bars as they stood on the outside runner board. They clung to the side of the car for dear life as the force of the ups and downs and curves tested their leg strength.

The conductor clanged a big brass bell as he approached every intersection, and let a young girl and boy stand next to him at the front of the car. He alternated putting his conductors' cap on each child and showed them how to strike the bell at just the right time; the passengers cheered, and the children's faces beamed with pride. People waiting in cars at intersections waved and smiled at the passing cable car. On a curve at the corner of Powell and Jackson streets, a man in a second-story apartment had a similar bell hanging in his open window. The riders hailed and when he showed up at the last minute to ring it; he hung his head out of the window and waved to the passing cable car. The gravitational pull was strong as the cable car chucked up the steep inclines. At the top of the highest hill, a beautiful vista of the entire San Francisco Bay was laid out in front of them with the strong orange-rust hues of the Golden Gate Bridge on the left and blue water under sunny skies to the right. The white and gray fog had finally crawled back out to sea. The speedy ride down the hill was a thrill for the passengers, but not for other drivers on the road unfamiliar with navigating hills in San Francisco. They couldn't hide their panicked faces as they scurried out of the way of the seemingly unstoppable wheeled behemoth.

As they passed by the Cable Car Museum, some passengers jumped off to take a tour and see the actual workings of the cable mechanism under the streets, which moved the cars along. Jenae and Neve stayed on and passed by Chinatown before getting off at Union Square. They caught a new cable car line after workers on a rotating platform had turned it around. On the ride to Ghirardelli Square, they passed Nob Hill and Russian Hill. They caught a glimpse of Lombard Street, dubbed the crookedest street in the country, with cars gingerly making their way down steep turns.

"Hey, have you been here before? Ghirardelli sounds familiar. Is this where you got the chocolates that we had in Hawaii?" Jenae asked.

"Yes, I must confess that I love chocolate and I think we should go in to buy some more. I am fresh out. We can have it with hot tea later on tonight."

They got enough chocolates in many flavors to share with their hosts and for late night dipping. On the way back to the Wharf, they stopped in the Buena Vista Restaurant for a drink at the ornate oak bar. Jenae ordered their famous Irish Coffee, and Neve ordered a tall Guinness on tap.

"So, what do you think of San Francisco so far?"

"Today has been really fun, and the weather has been great. I guess January is a good month to come. I was here once before in July on vacation, and it was just as Mark Twain said; 'The coldest winter I ever spent was a summer in San Francisco.' I have a good sweatshirt collection from that visit."

"It was a bit chilly when Karl and I visited last summer, but we still had a blast. I want to take you to a cool restaurant on the Wharf. I made reservations for an early dinner."

Neve followed the hostess to a prime booth facing full-length windows with the bay directly in sight.

"Wow, this is an amazing view!" Jenae said.

"I wanted to make it a special night for you, Jenae. How could you turn down living in San Francisco with a view like this? Look, there are boats passing by with their lights reflecting on the bay."

"It's very romantic, thank you," Jenae said.

A seasoned waitress took their dinner orders and brought them a basket of sourdough bread with butter, along with their drinks. Neve stayed with beer and Jenae tried a Tequila Sunrise because it looked pretty on the drink menu.

They both still felt a strong connection to each other, and the sexual tension had been building up all day. The big booth overlooking the bay was the most privacy they had so far on this trip. They snuggled close to each other in the middle of the booth seat and looked into each other's eyes while stealing kisses when no one was watching. Neve kept his left arm around Jenae's shoulders and his right hand rested on her upper right thigh. They were close enough to exchange whispers between soft kisses and giggles.

A shared appetizer of crab cakes filled Jenae up and she had to take her entire fish entrée home in a doggy bag. Neve devoured his steak and lobster platter without hesitation.

"How can you eat that much? You barely have any fat on you," Jenae asked.

"Good genes, I guess. I exercise a lot too; between running and speed boxing I burn a lot of calories. Besides, my cousin's cooking has been geared toward her kids' tastes and I've been looking forward to eating a real adult meal. That should hold me over for another week." Neve lifted his shirt and patted his flat six-pack abs.

Jenae blushed, remembering what the rest of his body looked like without clothes on.

"Should we get out of here? I see people waiting for tables out front. I think we've overstayed our welcome."

They stopped at a secluded bench along the waterfront to watch the fog roll in. The humid air and long, deep foghorns in the distance created a romantic eeriness that Jenae had never experienced before. Her feelings overcame her inhibitions as she sat on Neve's lap and held his face in her hands. She kissed his face and firmly pushed her warm, moist tongue into his mouth and the world began to spin for her again. Neve felt every curve of Jenae's hips as his pants protruded and pressed against her legs.

"Hey, what's that?" Jenae snickered.

"It's my friend. I think he wants to come out to play."

"Oh, really?" Jenae reached down and softly held his pulsating bulge.

"Yeah, he's been really lonely and is really happy to see you."

"Tell him he has to wait a little longer until I get you home."

"That's going to be a really long, hard drive for him."

"Hmm. How long and how hard?"

Jenae and Neve didn't make it out of the parking lot before steaming up the windshield of her brother's soft-top convertible and maneuvering around the stick shift of the fast, little car. Jenae's long, bare legs stretched up to the dashboard; one rested on the edge of the door with her painted toenails sticking out of a crack between the window and the soft top. Neve heaved between, while nuzzling her smoothest flesh. Jenae wanted to say that she loved him, but was scared. She was only sure of one thing . . . she wanted to belong to Neve and nobody else.

———◆◇◆———

Jenae found herself playing the third wheel at a Thai restaurant the next night in Palo Alto with her brother and his girlfriend, Sandy.

"So how do you like the Bay Area? Have you gotten a chance to look around?" Sandy asked.

"Yesterday I spent the day in the city with my New Zealand friend, Neville—he goes by Neve. We took in the usual tourist sites," Jenae replied.

"How long is Neve here for? I thought you were coming out to decide if you wanted to go to business school here," Brother asked.

"Well, I suppose it's a little bit of both. Neve and I have been in contact since last summer in Hawaii. He moved here not too long ago. Don't worry, I plan to drive to the city by myself and check out the university tomorrow," Jenae said.

"I see. Don't get sidetracked by some guy with an accent. Waiter? Can I get some more peanut sauce for this satay? I love the peanut sauce more than the chicken," Brother added.

"Did you happen to drive by the Marina? That's where I live. It's where all the young, hot single people stay in the city, and they have really cool neighborhood restaurants," Sandy said as she pointed to her own face and make a double click with her throat.

"Not yet. I can stop by tomorrow to check it out, though," Jenae said.

"I'll tell you what. If you come by after three in the afternoon, I should be done with my work calls, and I can show you around. We can grab a glass of vino," Sandy offered.

Sandy prided herself on making connections between people, and was the epicenter of all of her friend groups. She was a great conversationalist and earned every expensive meal by making her dates feel important by listening to their mundane stories with loud laughs and engaged sparkling blue eyes. But Sandy really liked Jenae's brother and was willing to entertain Jenae to gain brownie points with him and to see where their relationship might lead.

"Your brother may be busy, but he is not cheap. He takes me to the nicest restaurants and the best parties." Sandy winked at her date across the table and often mistook money equating to love.

"I do what I can," Brother said.

"But I'm still working on his wardrobe. His uniform is a white shirt, blue jeans, no socks, and black wingtip shoes. I wish he would go shopping with me just one time."

"Consider that an upgrade, Sandy. Growing up, he and our three brothers came to the breakfast every morning basically naked, only wearing their tighty-whities." Jenae shook her head and gave a mischievous grin.

"In our defense, we wore Speedos most of the summer. So, what's the difference?" Brother asked.

Driving a stick shift Alpha Romeo up and down the hills of San Francisco took Jenae's clutch skills to a new level. Before leaving Palo Alto, she looked up the addresses of the university and hospitals and plotted them out on her map to plan her most efficient route. The university was a gem in the middle of a big city. The campus donned a majestic cathedral, and the grounds were manicured with aromatic flowering bushes lining the sidewalks. Jenae lifted her face to the sun overhead and took her jacket off in the temperate climate. A little breeze from the bay blew a sense of calmness over Jenae as she imagined herself in a silky cocoon of the campus. She approached the administration building for graduate studies and stepped over an engraved plaque on the stone sidewalk near the cathedral. It was familiar . . . Monsignor Desaix. She had a great-uncle by that name.

"Hi, I wanted to come by to say 'hello.' I'm Jenae and I've applied for admission to the MBA program here. I would be a transfer student from Texas." She introduced herself to the woman in charge of the graduate business program. Jenae had sent an application to the school just two weeks earlier and had included a short essay for consideration of a fellowship scholarship.

"Hello Jenae, you have impeccable timing. Is this you?" The program director smiled and waved her application packet in the air.

Jenae leaned over the desk and turned a light shade of red. "Yep, that's me. The nurse who wants to get her MBA."

"Excellent. Well, I can say that we are very interested in having you in our program, and I'm intrigued that you are coming from a nursing background."

"Yes, I like the university's four-day week schedule with evening class options. If I am accepted, I'll be working my way through on the weekends at one of the hospitals in town."

After an informal interview with the director, Jenae walked around the campus and ended up in the student center. It was empty because everyone was on semester break. At the campus store, she scooped chocolate-covered raisins into thin plastic baggy and grabbed a can of Diet Coke before she headed for the register. Alone in a dark corner of the student lounge, Jenae pretended to read pamphlets while she formulated a pro/con list in her mind for moving to San Francisco. Neve was at the top of the pro list.

—◈—

"Yes, I'm at home. All finished with my sales calls." Sandy sold software for a large company in Silicon Valley. She told stories and used acronyms that only she and her geeky, tech-savvy customers could comprehend.

"OK, I'll make my way over to the Marina after I finish checking out this hospital." Jenae placed the receiver back on the phone hook in the reception area of the biggest medical center she had ever seen. The buildings ran for blocks and the view of the Golden Gate Bridge from the cafeteria was amazing. She drove past Golden Gate Park where runners and bikers moved along paths throughout the vast green lawns.

⊷◉⊶

Sandy stood in front of her four-story apartment building and waved Jenae into a scarce parking spot on the street.

"How was your day? Have you decided to move here yet? If you do, you'll become an expert in parallel parking!" Sandy said enthusiastically.

"I really like it here and everything seems to be pointing me to do it. Plus, my car is an automatic and would be able to handle these hills."

"Let me show you around my neighborhood. You'd love living down here."

Sandy walked Jenae to the Greek Deli, where she leaned in the doorway to say hello to a large smiling man slicing beef behind the counter.

"Good afternoon, Sandy! Do you need some meats?"

"Not yet, Niko! I'll be back, though. This is my friend, Jenae. She is going to move here. I am showing her around," Sandy said.

"Hey Niko. It's nice to meet you," Jenae said.

"Come by anytime, Jenae, and I will give you some free samples."

"Thanks, Niko!" Sandy half turned with a wave as she continued walking down the sidewalk.

They ended up in at a local Italian restaurant with a small brick patio that gave them glances of the bay through the colorful apartment houses of the marina.

"I'm glad that you came to visit now because I am leaving for Europe in a few weeks and will be gone for at least a month. My studio apartment will be empty, and you can stay in it while I'm gone if you want."

"Wow, that is really generous of you. I might take you up on that. I have a lot to do to get things in order, but hopefully it will work out in my favor."

"So, tell me about this Neve character. Do you think he's 'mister right' or just 'mister right now'?"

"I think he may be the one. But everything is so complicated with him coming from a foreign country. He thinks it's easy to work here and get a visa, but I've heard that it's very difficult. I'm willing to give it a try if he is. Who knows?"

Chapter 6

Luck

The flight on an American 757 plane headed back to Dallas-Fort Worth was less exciting than Jenae's trip to San Francisco a week earlier, if not downright depressing. She missed Neve already and had lots of thoughts about their future after spending almost every day together. Her decisions over the next few weeks would determine the trajectory of her life. Either she could stay comfortable in Dallas with her dog, Gremlin, or she could take the gamble and move to San Francisco and possibly be with her future husband. Neve was not at all interested in moving to Texas because his brother was planning to share an apartment with him when he arrived in the States. Hamish played bass guitar, sang in a band and practiced a lot of yoga. Hamish was much older and nurtured Neve as a father, not a brother.

JT, Jenae's workmate, had offered to take Gremlin long term and make her part of their family. His children were upset that they had to give the dog back to Jenae after her week away. They'd grown accustomed to playing with her in their tree house and sleeping with her at night. Gremmie looked cute dressed up, too.

Jenae resigned from her weekend night position at the medical center and signed on to the per diem pool so that she could work the day shift. The green-eyed bandit had made bail, and she didn't feel safe working at night with a skeleton staff anymore. Detectives hadn't returned her calls about her bracelet, and she assumed that it was clean—that they hadn't found any tracking device inside. She did want it returned for sentimental reasons, but was still confused about who had given it to her. It was a nice memory of her summer in Hawaii.

Staffing the day surgery center meant driving in the dark and showing up to work before the break of dawn; but getting home by midday and sleeping in her own bed at night was a nice tradeoff. Jenae learned to drink coffee after spending time with Neve. He had a cultural pension to drink tea with milk, but also embraced coffee—the American way. The morning drives downtown were dark and lonely, but the smell and taste of a warm cup of joe woke her up and calmed her down at the same time.

"Hello, my name is Jenae and I'm your nurse this morning. I'll get you ready for surgery. I'm going to grab a few things to prep you and get your IV started and, then I'll be back to ask you some questions and have you sign some paperwork. While I'm getting that, you can change into this hospital gown." She held up a thin, cotton blue and green garment with long strings and holes for the arms.

A tall, lean man accompanied by his wife, seated on the bed, smiled sheepishly and nodded.

"Do I take everything else off?" the patient asked.

"Yes, everything off except the gown for surgery. I'll be right back," Jenae replied as she closed the room door behind her. Jenae returned with her arms full of paperwork, blankets, and IV supplies. She held a specimen cup out to the patient and said, "do you think you can fill this? We need a urine sample from you."

The patient stood up to walk to the bathroom with his gown on and the bottom-half of his derriere was exposed because he was so tall.

"Is the gown supposed to fit like this?" He covered his crotch area with his cupped hands while his wife stood by and chuckled.

"Oh no, I'm so sorry. That looks like a shirt on you. You didn't look that tall sitting down. Here, wrap this around your waist when you get out of bed." Jenae handed him a warming blanket that he wore like a sarong. Jenae unwrapped a shaving and iodine swabbing kit on the bedside table. She gingerly worked around the boney protrusions of the patient's knee with a razor, careful not to nick his skin.

"Is this the first time you've had your legs shaved?" Jenae asked the patient.

"Well, there was this one Halloween where . . ." The patient's wife stopped him and warned that it was too much information.

After the knee was triple cleaned with antiseptic wash, Jenae easily placed an 18-gauge needle into a "garden hose" vein in his arm. Even though the patient looked away, he winced and yelped when the needle poked his skin. The surgeon and anesthesiologist walked into the room together with great confidence, as if they were wearing halos. The surgeon marked the knee that he would be working on with a magic marker and explained the full procedure to the patient. The anesthesiologist explained all the risks associated with general anesthesia, including severe disability and death. After consent forms were signed, the transport worker waiting in the hallway peeked around the corner of the door and signaled Jenae.

"Hey, is the patient ready to go to the operating room?"

"Almost. I need to give him a pre-op med and gather his things."

"Is this guy who I think he is? Is he really tall?"

"Yeah, why?"

The transporter jumped and gasped when he caught a glimpse of the patient lying in bed talking to his wife.

"You really don't know who that is? You don't recognize his name?" He held his head with both hands.

"Nope, never heard of him, never seen him."

"He is the star player for the Dallas Mavericks! I have his jersey. Oh my God, this is crazy. He is my hero."

"I'm happy for you, but I only go to Ranger baseball games, and I couldn't name any of those players either. I only go because one of my patients in Hawaii last summer was a recruiter for them and he leaves me tickets at WILL CALL for almost every home game. He's a great guy," Jenae said.

"LUCKY!" the transporter said.

"The last game wasn't so lucky. My brother came to visit and I had four tickets. We got there early and the first thousand fans to arrive got a promo gift of a small wooden bat. It was about as long as a wooden spoon you cook with, but it had some girth and weight to it. Anyway, those early fans started drinking a lot of beer on a hot evening and wanted to fight. Bats were flying and blood splattered everywhere. A whole bunch of people got ejected before the third inning. Lots of fun," Jenae explained.

"Sounds exciting! We just boo and throw warm beer at basketball games."

The transporter skipped with glee while he pushed his basketball hero to the operating room. Jenae remained unfazed because she had zero knowledge and less interest in the professional athlete scene in Dallas.

Although working at the day surgery center was a sweet gig, Jenae waited for a big sign that would tell her to move to California. She anticipated that she'd have to get big student loans to pay for tuition at a private university, and apartments in San Francisco cost double of what she was used to paying in Texas. She'd checked into apartment rentals while she was there, and virtually nobody accepted dogs. She didn't know if she could part ways with her doggy, even though her friends had offered to give Gremlin a better life than Jenae ever could.

Jenae's MBA friends weren't keen on the idea of Jenae moving to San Francisco. But Kristine and Kyle backed off from deterring her decision. They were preoccupied with one another since they had started dating; shortly after Jenae had introduced them. Her business school tutors pretended to protest the most—just to make her feel guilty for wanting to leave them.

A week after returning from her trip to the Bay Area, Jenae opened a letter from the university in San Francisco. It read:

"We are pleased to inform you that you have been accepted into the Spring Class of 1989. We are also delighted to award you with a fellowship scholarship, which covers 75% of tuition."

Jenae's heart exploded as her head spun. She jumped uncoordinatedly in the air, pumping her fists up and down. Her neighbor at the mailbox gave her a thumbs up and a big smile. "Congratulations!" As she sprinted up the stairs to her apartment, she could only think of calling Neve as quickly as she could. "Hi Neve, I have some good news. I'm moving to San Francisco!"

⋯◦⋯

Life entered acceleration mode, like she was launched into space. Jenae immediately registered to continue her MBA in San Francisco and started calling hospitals for interviews. She reserved a U-Haul trailer to hook on the back of her Camry and sold her king-sized bed to JT for a very good price. He was willing to take it off her hands as long as it included Gremlin in the deal. Neve was elated that she would agree to move to California for him, and he booked a ticket back to Dallas to help her move and drive out.

"I'm really excited about driving across half of the country. Can we take Route 66 like in the movie 'Easy Rider?' I love Dennis Hopper," Neve asked Jenae.

"You are really into the hippie vibe, aren't you? How do you know about that movie?"

"I guess I was influenced by my older brother, Hamish. He's into the music scene of that time. Luckily, he never got into the drugs, though."

"I can't wait to meet him. He sounds like a cool old guy," Jenae joked.

"He'll be in San Francisco when we arrive. I secured an apartment in Marin County for him and me, I heard that's where a lot of musicians and celebrities live. We should get settled in there before I come to move you out."

"This will be an adventure for sure. Promise me one thing on our drive out to California," Jenae said.

"Sure, what?"

"When we are driving at night, we find the best night sky for viewing stars—and we make a wish together each time we see a shooting star."

"Sounds amazing," Neve said.

Chapter 7
Route 66

The smallest trailer available at the truck rental place attached easily to the metal ball on the backside of Jenae's Camry. Neve had arrived in Dallas two days ahead of the epic drive out west to California and was chomping at the bit to get the road trip started. His muscles swelled as he loaded small furniture and boxes full of clothes and kitchenware into the tagalong caboose.

"What do you want me to do with Gremlin's bowl and toys that we found in the closet?" Neve asked Jenae.

"I don't know. Maybe I'll leave it for my neighbor; she has a new puppy." Jenae's eyes filled with tears, and she knew she had to keep moving forward just to get through the pain of leaving her dog, Gremmie, behind. She'd taken Gremlin to work the week earlier and gave her one last kiss and hug before handing her over to her new owner. Gremlin was excited to see JT again, which took a little bit of the sting out of leaving her. She knew JT's kids would be thrilled to have her as a part of their family.

Neve put his arm around her shoulder, and Jenae buried her face in his chest.

"I'm sorry this is so hard for you. I wish you could've brought her with us."

"Me too. She was my first real responsibility as an adult. But it wouldn't be fair to keep her cooped up in the city."

"Maybe you can get a new dog when you get settled."

"No, I won't get another dog until I'm in a permanent home with a family."

"You know that I love dogs. We can pick one out together someday."

The Camry, with trailer in tow, left the parking lot of the apartment without any fanfare. Jenae had marked the route to Amarillo on a big map from AAA where they would pick up the famous Route 66. Jenae had prepared her vehicle by taking it for an oil change and tire rotation the day before, so she was surprised when they stopped for gas for the first time and the oil light had turned red.

"Pop the hood and I'll check the oil stick," Neve said as he finished pumping gas next to eighteen-wheel semis.

"OK, I'm going to run in and get a soda. Do you want one?"

"Sure, but none of that diet stuff. It tastes like a bucket of chemicals." Neve pulled the dipstick, wiped it clean and placed it back into the oil reservoir. No oil registered on the stick when he pulled it out again. He wiped it again and repeated the process—still no oil. Neve turned toward Jenae and hollered.

"Uh, Jenae, wait up." He jogged to the front of the super gas station.

"Do you need something else?" Jenae asked.

"Yeah, a bunch of liters of oil. Are you sure you got the oil changed? Maybe the car has a leak."

"Let's fill it up and check for a puddle. I bet those yahoos at the service station emptied it and forgot to refill it. I've never had a problem with it before."

"I'm shocked that we ran on no oil for three hundred miles without the engine seizing up; we're pulling that trailer, too."

"She's a good car!" Jenae's intuition was correct, no oil leak.

Neve took over driving and took notice of the yellow Post-it Note that Jenae had stuck on the windshield. It said, "Keep Right." Jenae fiddled with the radio knobs to find an AM station that played music. A static sound turned to a faint Glen Campbell song, "Wichita Lineman."

"Hey, this is about the town I grew up in."

"How far away is Wichita from here?"

"Two states north in Kansas; we won't be going through there this trip. Although my girlfriends from high school would love to meet you."

A billboard on the highway advertised a restaurant that tempted customers with a 72-ounce steak dinner eating challenge. The steak was free if it was consumed in one hour. Neve pointed to the sign and promised to come back and try the challenge.

"Do you know how much 72 ounces is? That's four and a half pounds of beef!" Jenae challenged.

"No problem. That's two kilos, yeah? After a good run and workout, I bet I could do it. Then I wouldn't need to eat for a week. Like a lion after a kill on the Serengeti."

"You're so practical."

Route 66 took them through Albuquerque and a petrified forest before stopping in Winslow, Arizona.

"I've always wanted to come to a corner in Winslow, Arizona. You know the Eagles band, right?" Jenae asked.

"Of course, they're iconic."

"'Take it Easy' was my favorite song one summer in high school. I think it played every hour over the radio while I was a lifeguard. I never got tired of it," Jenae said.

"You have good taste."

"Who is your favorite musician?"

"Oh, Jimi Hendrix for sure," Neve said.

"Who?" Jenae asked.

"He was a rock blues electric guitarist and singer who died of an overdose when we were kids, but my brother, Hamish, had all his albums and I grew up on 'Hey Joe' and 'Purple Haze.' He was an incredible talent. What a waste. I wish I could've seen him in concert."

The elevation to Flagstaff in the dark was a stark contrast to the hot, dry desert they'd just traversed. They parked between tall pine trees at a roadside hotel, and Neve stretched his arms out wide and leaned back while he took in a big breath of fresh air. They each lay down on their own bed in the double-double room. It was the only room left at the hotel, but Jenae and Neve were relieved to have a spot to rest their heads until the morning.

"Good morning, beautiful. Are you hungry for breakfast?" Neve gently gazed into Jenae's bleary eyes and set a tray of pastries, fruit, and coffee next to her on her bed. He gave her a kiss on the cheek.

"Oh, good morning. I guess I didn't hear you get up. You brought me breakfast in bed. How romantic. Did you get that from the hotel? It looks pretty good."

"They didn't have diet soda or vegemite toast, so this'll have to do," Neve said.

"Are you up for a detour to the Grand Canyon? It'll add at least a half day onto our travel, but we aren't in a time crunch; are we?" Jenae asked.

"Hell yeah. Of course, I want to see the famous Grand Canyon. You're making my American adventure dreams come true. I feel like this could be a honeymoon trip."

Jenae blushed and pretended she didn't hear his references to marriage.

Neve went for a six-mile run along a path through the pine trees while Jenae showered, dressed, and plotted out directions on a map for the day.

The drive to the canyon was stop and go because they got stuck behind tourist buses on the two-lane road. A pit-stop at a local gas station to pick up sandwiches and use the restroom took way longer than Jenae had budgeted. Desert sand, cacti, and one roadrunner bird were the only sights until they reached the massive crevasse. The whole earth opened up before their eyes as they drove closer to a colorful wavy hole in the ground in front of them.

"Wow! This is so beautiful and magnificent. Picture books don't do it justice," Neve said.

"It's amazing, isn't it? I came here once on a family vacation when I was a kid, but I didn't appreciate the grandness of the canyon. I was a petulant pre-teen."

"You can't see the whole thing without moving your head back and forth and scanning the horizon."

"Look at all the striations of rock and dirt all the way down. The Colorado River looks like a tiny trickle of a stream. I wonder what it is like to raft down there."

Jenae and Neve found a picnic spot far enough away from the edge but close enough to take in the view while they ate their turkey and cheese sandwiches on French bread. They lay down next to each other on their blanket in the shade and breathed in the fresh piney air.

"This reminds me of moments in my childhood. See that commercial plane flying high in the sky?" Neve asked.

"Yeah, it doesn't look like it is going very fast from down here," Jenae said.

"When I was about four or five years old, we lived near the airport in Christchurch and planes flew over the house quite often. I would lay in the grass on summer days and watch them pass overhead with my imaginary friend, Jerry."

"Who? So, you just hung out with your imaginary friend in the backyard?" Jenae asked.

"Except, I still don't think he was imaginary. He was real somehow because he taught me all about airplanes and how the speed over the wing is higher than under the wing, which creates lower pressure and gives it lift. I loved going out to talk to him. He sure seemed real to me."

"How long did he hang around?"

"He was only with me for a few weeks, maybe a month, but I distinctly remember that he taught me Bernoulli's principle in physics. How would I know that as a wee child? My mom got concerned that some old man from the neighborhood was sneaking into our backyard."

"Well, I believe you. My niece had an imaginary friend, Nancy. We had to leave a spot in the car for her to ride in the front seat."

Jenae fed Neve red grapes one by one and gave him a soft kiss after each one entered his mouth. All they could hear was the rustling of pine needles overhead and the sound of naughty whispers in each other's ears. Neve's earlobes tickled with the brushing of Jenae's pouty lips. Neve's hands roamed under her shirt on Jenae's bare skin as he skillfully removed her bra and took control. Neve expertly linked heaven with earth for both of them. Lying naked, face-to-face, and hip to thigh, they blended in with the beauty of the moment—only for nature to witness.

◆

The Las Vegas strip took the love-struck pair to the opposite end of the spectrum, from nature to a large concrete boulevard with palatial hotels and glimmering lights. Jenae had only heard of the Flamingo Hotel from her friends; it was one of the original hotels built in the desert. Not only did it have inviting pools with cabanas, but the resort had a real-life flamingo exhibit, like in a zoo. They stopped at the fabulous pink neon marquee designed to resemble the rounded body feathers of a flamingo to check in. Valet parked the Camry and trailer without hesitation. They were familiar with travel trailers stopping in Las Vegas on long moves. The front desk upgraded them to a corner suite on the top floor overlooking the strip.

"I can't believe this room is so cheap. I mean, the view is outstanding, and it is so big," Neve said.

"They probably made a bet that we'll spend lots of money in the casino and restaurants. Do you like to gamble?" Jenae asked.

"I only like to play blackjack because it has the best odds of winning. I never plan on walking away with any money in my pocket when I'm on the casino floor, and I rarely do."

"The slot machines are fun, but my hands always feel grimy after plugging nickels into the machine," Jenae said.

"Nickels?" Neve asked.

"Yeah, five cents at a time. It lasts longer. I'm usually a lucky person, but not in gambling. I did win a big pot playing Keno at a restaurant one time," Jenae said.

Neve called the concierge and booked a dinner variety show reservation in the hotel. A comedian and magician were the main entertainment; rib eye, baked potato, and shrimp cocktail were on the menu. They sat in a booth with another couple facing the stage as women in feathery sequined bodysuits served them dinner and drinks. The middle-aged couple was celebrating their twentieth anniversary and drew a lot of attention from the entertainers. Jenae got called up on stage, was blind folded and placed against a target board while one magician threw knives around her body. She was terrified because it seemed so real. Neve told her afterward how the trick worked, and she was relieved that she was never in any danger.

After the show, they left the hotel and walked the strip past sparkling neon signs and vendors selling trinkets and passing out pamphlets for late night strip shows.

"Hey, if the work visa doesn't work out for you, you could audition for the Thunder from Down Under. You have the hot body for it," Jenae teased.

"I think that job is reserved for Aussies only, thank God."

Chapter 8

Arrival

The drive through the Mojave Desert was longer and more boring than Neve had anticipated, but Bakersfield gave them a little bit of hope that they would reach the Bay Area before nightfall. Traffic was torture in Jenae's book. Her body quaked as she tried to sit still in the driver's seat. She ran her fingers through her hair and sighed because she couldn't go any faster with a sea of red taillights in stop and go traffic. Neve had fallen asleep in the reclined shotgun seat and drooled into a soft travel pillow leaned against the passenger door. Jenae stretched out her long, left leg onto the dashboard in front of her and remembered her moment of weakness the last time she was in a parked car with Neve in San Francisco. She longed for a cigarette, even though she had given up the habit years ago.

"We made it!" Jenae pulled into a U Haul store parking lot that had storage units and trailer returns.

"Let's do this fast." Neve moved stealthily and efficiently as he relocated most of the boxes into a closet-sized storage unit all by himself. Jenae helped him with the furniture, and they were back on the road to Neve and Hamish's apartment within the hour. She felt free and energized. Neve changed the radio in the Camry to a local rock station, tapped his hand on the dashboard, and lifted his heel to the beat of an Eric Clapton song. His head nodded as he sang, "Layla."

"I called Hamish from the pay phone back there, and he's expecting us in the next thirty to forty minutes. He's picking up some Chinese food for us to eat when we get there."

"What a good big brother. I can't wait to meet him. Ugh, I'm starved," Jenae said.

"Me too, I could tackle that 72-ounce steak back in Amarillo about now."

"I'm so thankful that we made this journey together. And thanks for letting me sleep in your bed tonight. It won't be awkward with your brother, will it?"

"Oh, no. He obviously knows all about you and is really excited to meet you."

"Good, I think it's too late to try to get the keys for Sandy's apartment."

"Can her friend meet you at the apartment tomorrow?"

"I'm pretty sure she can. I'll call her from your place tonight to make sure."

"Give yourself some time to recover. I didn't realize how big America was until going on this road trip. And we only covered half of it."

"I'd like to rest, but I want to stop into some hospitals to apply for jobs tomorrow, too. Classes start in two weeks, my head is spinning, and I can't believe I'm in San Francisco. It seems like this all happened so fast."

Hamish greeted the road-worn couple outside of the two-bedroom apartment nestled up against Mt. Tamalpais. Upon first meeting Hamish, he didn't look the way Jenae expected him to. She could tell that Neve and Hamish were brothers, but they looked different enough that they could've been half-brothers. Hamish gave both of them hugs. With a big smile, he invited them to sit at the kitchen table covered with white and red boxes filled with white rice, Kung Pao Chicken, and Beef Broccoli. Hamish handed them each paper-covered chopsticks included in the food delivery and said, "Dig in." The threesome clinked Tsingtao beer bottles together and Hamish shared a toast. "We made it. Here's to a future of success, love, abundance, and beautiful memories—and no eggs. Neve told me you were allergic to eggs."

⊷◇⊶

The drive over the Golden Gate Bridge by herself the next day was exhilarating and terrifying for Jenae. After paying the toll, all she could think about was veering off the side of the bridge and endlessly falling into the cold choppy waters below. Her hands sweated on the steering wheel and her knees were weak until she reached solid ground at the Presidio. Once she arrived in the city, the scenic views of the hills against the bay took her mind off her anxiety attack as she looked for streets to lead her to Sandy's apartment in the Marina District.

It was another warm sunny day in the middle of winter and Jenae sat out on the front curb of the apartment as she waited for Sandy's friend, Annie, to show up to let her in and give her the key. Annie lived around the corner from Sandy and dated one of Sandy's friends from Portland, Oregon.

"Hi! Thanks for coming over and letting me in."

"Sure, no problem. I mostly work from home. I would have been here earlier, but I was on a business call."

The young professionals in San Francisco seemed more put together than in any other town that Jenae had lived in. They were polished inside and out with designer clothing, manicured hands and flawless complexions. They were also fit and vibrant because they ate a lot of salads and little red meat.

"Sandy said that you'll be staying here for a month while she is gallivanting around Europe. Do you know where you want to live after that?" Annie asked.

"No plans yet, I need to find a job first and I suppose I'll want to live near the hospital and school. The university is really close to Golden Gate Park and the big medical center is over there, too."

"Well, my roommate is moving out of my apartment in a few weeks, and we have a great two-bedroom place just around the corner. Let me know if you'd be interested in taking her spot. I would split the rent with you right down the middle."

"OK, cool. I appreciate the offer. Let me figure more out and I'll get back to you."

"You have my number. Give me a call anytime," Annie replied.

Jenae dragged her suitcases up the curved marble staircase to the second-floor studio apartment. It was cute, pink and had a view of the bay, but it was very small. Jenae opened her suitcases on the floor in front of the bay window and cranked her head to the side to see a boat floating by in the distance. She opened the window and smelled fish as she lay down on a fluffy down comforter on the brass bed. There were no other seating choices, except for pillows on the hardwood floor.

The drive up and down the hills of San Francisco was easier with automatic transmission in her Camry, and Jenae felt comfortable navigating some neighborhoods. She drove past the campus to check for rental signs at apartment buildings, but she didn't see any that looked appealing. She stopped into a small hospital nearby to fill out an application. It was in a great neighborhood and when she inquired at HR, they basically hired her on the spot as long as she passed a background check. They were thrilled that she had experience with HIV/AIDS patients at the medical center in Dallas because one of the wards at the hospital cared almost exclusively for AIDS patients. Unfortunately, the new disease that hit mostly gay men and IV drug users was usually fatal. Although local biomedical pharmaceutical companies were working on it, there were no effective treatments for the autoimmune infection that caused cancers and organ failure.

On the way to the big medical center, she had some extra time before her interview, and she stopped in to visit the arboretum in Golden Gate Park. A Japanese Tea Garden was nearby with Ginkgo trees out front, and Jenae made a mental note to come back when the cherry blossoms were in full bloom.

Nurses were in high demand in San Francisco, and the medical center was happy that Jenae wanted to work twelve-hour weekend shifts to fit around her full time MBA schedule. She planned to juggle shifts at both hospitals to make ends meet in her new fancy city with prices to match.

<hr>

Informal orientation for business school started at a bar on the Wharf the evening before classes started. Male students were dressed in dress slacks, business button downs, and ties. They tried hard to impress the female students who wore business casual attire, which equated to a cute dress with high heels. Countries from all around the world were represented in the class. Jenae had never met anyone from Iceland before, but four very blond blue-eyed students from Reykjavik explained that Iceland was green, and Greenland was icy. An Australian tennis player boasted that his country was superior to New Zealand when Jenae mentioned Neve.

A group of Middle-Eastern men from Palestine, Morocco, Lebanon, and Syria laughed the loudest and appeared to have the most fun. An Israeli female student joined in as they talked about their favorite dishes from home. An over-served student from Hong Kong brought two fists full of shots and handed them out to the group where Jenae was standing. He spoke fluent English, but toasted the group in Chinese, "Gon Bay!" The group clinked their shot glasses together, "Gon Bay!" Jenae tried to slam the clear jet fuel down her gullet, but her throat clenched, not allowing it to be consumed. She received a resounding "Boo!" from her chiding social group whom all managed to swallow theirs with enthusiasm. Her face turned a slight shade of red, but knew that she would avoid a certain hangover the next morning.

Jenae got the idea that most of her classmates were extremely wealthy, or they came to the university in the U.S. on their own government's dime. Many countries valued American education and found it convenient to send their citizens to a private school if they hadn't developed their own higher educational system in a certain curriculum like business. Networking opportunities abroad, especially in business in an emerging tech era were priceless.

A special star sticker was placed on the handful of student nametags that were granted fellowships. The group of six students was instructed to find one another and get to know each other because they would be working together on projects for the professors. All the distinguished fellows were Americans who worked full-time while attending the program. With that distinction, Jenae didn't feel so special or smart for her scholarship achievement, but she was grateful nonetheless because she wouldn't be in debt at the end of the program like some of her classmates.

Chapter 9

Cloudy Skies

Neve and his brother, Hamish, initially had success finding odd construction jobs around the Bay Area because they knew a few Kiwis who had relocated and were willing to let them work under the table. They started with a real estate investor who hired them to paint, lay carpet, and landscape his flips like they had done before in Christchurch. But only getting paid a low hourly wage was demoralizing for the hard work that they put into the jobs because they knew firsthand how much money the investor was clearing after the flip. Hamish had connected with local musicians and played backup bass guitar at least once a week. Neve considered himself a roadie because he moved the equipment in and out of venues for various bands but only cleared two, maybe three beers a night for his efforts. Hamish loved playing with talented artists, and the excitement kept him buzzing into the early morning hours. He had insomnia and worried about finances the rest of the nights of the week.

"We're basically living on our savings, and it's going fast," Neve said.

"I thought it would be so much easier finding work here. But this is such a huge area, and the travel time alone is prohibitive for a lot of the jobs offered to us," Hamish replied.

"I feel bad that I brought you out here. I obviously miscalculated the environment, and I'm a selfish jerk because I wanted to have a future here with Jenae," Neve said.

"Do you love her? I mean, you've had a few serious girlfriends already, but none that you seemed this keen on," Hamish asked.

"I've fallen for her pretty hard, and I can't see my future without her in it," Neve said.

"Do you think she loves you, too? She did relocate her life to be in the same metropolis as you."

"I think so? I hope so? She acts like she loves me."

"Are you ready to get married? You've known each other for what, seven months already?"

"Nah, I don't think that's a very good idea. We've been on different hemispheres for most of that time, and she's in the middle of grad school and working full-time. I'm sure she'd be too overwhelmed to get married now."

"But think about it, Neve. If we took a quick trip to Vegas, you two could get hitched, you could stay in the country legally and get a decent job, and you would have a great story to tell. And you could help your brother get work so we both could stay here."

"I do really want to marry Jenae, but I don't want to do it like that. I want us to have a proper wedding with all our family around us and when it's the right time for everybody. I can't do that to her. Just marry her for a green card? Are you serious, Hamish?"

"Hey, don't get mad at me. I'm just brainstorming over here, trying to salvage this shitty situation." Hamish cracked his knuckles with bulged eyes.

Neve left Hamish sitting on a big peach couch in their living room; he grabbed the phone, unplugged it from the wall in the kitchen, and took it to his bedroom. He called Jenae, but she couldn't talk because she was having a study session with her classmates. It had something to do with international relations and tariffs and treaties. Neve rifled through his wallet and found a card that Captain Deely from Seattle had given him at the motel bar in Christchurch. He paced back and forth and unbuttoned the top of his shirt as he studied the phone number. Neve firmly sat on the side of his bed, picked up the receiver, and dialed.

"Hello? Deely speaking."

"Hey, Captain Deely, this is Neve. I'm the guy that you met with my brother at the bar in Christchurch a few months ago. We were the ones with paint in our hair."

"Roger that, I remember you. Your accent gives you away. How are you guys doing? Did you make it to the States?"

"We sure did. I've been here a few months already and my brother came a few weeks after me. We're all settled in and trying to figure things out."

"Are you doing alright? Is there anything I can do to help you out? I remember you were interested in aviation."

"I heeded your advice and took a discovery flight with a local pilot in New Zealand before I came to the States. It was in a single-engine Cessna, and I had a lot of fun. It was a blast, actually."

"How's the work situation? Do you have time to spend a few days in Seattle?"

"Jobs are fleeting at best in my situation, and I'm just trying to keep my head above water at the moment. I don't have any obligations right now."

"It sounds like you have some free time. Why don't you fly up here and I can show you around my base. The commuter airlines have really cheap fares right now. We have some pretty cool military planes I could let you look at, and if you want, spend a night or two at my house. I'm sure my wife wouldn't mind. Bring your girlfriend; the two of you could look around Seattle and drive up to Everett and tour the big Boeing plant there."

"Wow, you just lifted my spirits. So, you are OK with us staying at your house? Americans are so much friendlier than Kiwis or Brits in general. I'll call Jenae and let you know what she says."

"OK, I fly out on another mission in two weeks, so the sooner, the better for me."

"Got it. I'll be in touch."

"Talk to you soon, Bud."

Hamish went to their small-town bar to get away from Neve and numb his nerves. He knew a female bartender who was sweet on him and poured him an unadvertised two-for-one special. Hamish would have proposed to the bartender if she didn't already have two young children and a husband.

Jenae called Neve back and thought it was a fabulous idea to check out Seattle together. She had Spring Break coming up and didn't plan to work extra shifts at the hospital during her time off. Her schedule had been so hectic and demanding that she and Neve were lucky to see each other one night a week.

"Let's get tickets for next week after my shift at the hospital," Jenae said.

"Sounds good. I'm looking forward to having you all to myself for a few days," Neve replied.

"I've missed you too, Neve. You wouldn't believe the time I spend reading and writing papers. I hope it'll all be worth it in the end."

"I know you are enjoying classes and hanging out with your classmates. Don't lie to make me feel better."

"I'm not lying. I wish we could live in the same neighborhood. You live in a beautiful area, but going across the Golden Gate Bridge seems like a road trip from the city, and paying a toll each time doesn't help either."

Jenae had moved into the vacant bedroom that Annie offered her in the Marina after Sandy returned from Europe. She rarely saw her new roommate, and most of Jenae's belongings remained boxed up in the garage. There was no room in the cabinets for Jenae's food, and she had a space big enough for a carton of milk in the refrigerator. Jenae basically only slept there between classes, studying at the library, and shifts at the hospital.

⸎

The morning flight from SFO to Seattle was short and sweet. Their cheap seats bought them backward facing seats, which made Jenae nauseous and dizzy throughout the flight. Jenae rented a car while Neve called Deely to let him know that they had arrived.

"Deely and his wife are expecting us for dinner at their house at six. I picked up a visitor's brochure, and it looks like there is a lot to see in Seattle today," Neve said.

"I hear Pike's Market is fun. The fishmongers throw whole fish back and forth over icy display cases. I saw it in a movie, "When Harry Met Sally," Jenae said.

"I remember that movie. Didn't she have an orgasm at a lunch table?"

"Well, she pretended."

"Have you ever faked it with me?"

"Hmm, let me think. I can't remember." Jenae smirked and handed the car rental agreement to the attendant.

Pike's Market didn't disappoint, but the weather was gray and gloomy as advertised. The iconic bright red "Public Market" sign over a green tin roof made Jenae feel like she was on a movie set. She and Neve held hands as they walked by buckets of fresh flowers, cases of whole fish, fruit stands and freshly baked goods. Specialty food shops, vintage book and craft stores offered a warm respite from the cool mist blowing off the Puget Sound.

"What kind of flowers do you like best?" Neve asked Jenae.

"I like the look of orange and yellow Gerber daisies, but my favorite smell is from little purple freesias. I like most flowers, just no gardenias. Yuck, the smell of gardenias makes me gag."

"I only know roses and dandelions, so I'll take your word that those are the best."

They walked further around the pier and found a restaurant with a water view.

"Do you mind putting our name on the list to eat here? It got five-star reviews for its clam chowder in the brochure. And you can stand inside where it's warm. I'm going to grab something. I'll be right back."

"Sure, not a problem."

Jenae visited the ladies' room and discovered why she was nauseous and cranky; her period came a few days early. She plugged a quarter into the tampon machine attached to the wall and turned the knob. Nothing came out. "Shit." She rummaged in the bottom of her purse and found another quarter. This time, the sanitary napkin machine spit out a small box. She fixed her face and fluffed her damp, mousy hair under the electric hand driers as best she could. Neve returned to the restaurant with a bouquet of flowers in newsprint paper and handed them to Jenae.

"They didn't have any Gerber daisies, but I think there are a few freesias in there. These are for you. Beautiful flowers for my beautiful girlfriend."

"Aw, they're lovely and they smell divine. Thank you." Jenae leaned in on her tiptoes and gave Neve a quick kiss on the cheek.

A young petite hostess shouted from her oak podium, "party for two, NAVE, NIV, NEV."

"It's Neve; like Steve." Neve corrected her with a shy smile.

"Ah, I've never seen that name before. I love your accent! Are you from England or something?" The waitress touched her ponytail and smiled with a sparkle in her eyes.

"No, try again. The southern hemisphere."

"Oh, I know, you're from Australia!"

"Nope, I'm from New Zealand. Have you heard of that country? It's right next to Australia."

"I think I have. Was Jurassic Park filmed there?"

Jenae rolled her eyes and cocked her head while watching her doting boyfriend flirt with a complete stranger. Neve turned heads with his movie star looks everywhere they went. His clothes always looked pressed and perfect because he had an ideal body with robust muscles and a lean waistline. He would look freshly manicured even after a week in the bush. His superman talent was focusing in on whomever he was talking to and making them feel like they were the only person in the room.

Jenae was annoyed, hungry, and felt frumpy. She decided that this lunch was the perfect time to ask him about their future together.

"So, how long have Deely and his wife been married? How'd they meet?" Jenae asked Neve.

"I think he said that he married his wife after she finished law school. Maybe last year, or two years ago. They dated in undergrad in Colorado, so they've been together for a long time."

"When do you see yourself getting married? Do you want children?" Jenae squinted her eyes.

"Whoa, are you mad at me? You seem pissed off," Neve replied.

"I just don't know what we are doing. You're living here without a real job. You're flirting with the waitress right in front of me, and I barely see you even though we live twenty miles away from each other."

"I see. Well, I want to get married when I'm sure it will work out longterm. I'm not certain that I want children, but I am willing to have an open-mind and compromise. If Deely and his wife can wait eight years before they got married, then I don't see the rush."

"Eight years? I'll just tell you right now that I'm not waiting eight years to marry anybody. My fertility clock is ticking, and I've never imagined my life without having my own children."

"I want to be with you, but I just don't know how." Neve bowed his head.

Jenae's shoulders slumped, her uterus cramped, and her stomach turned in knots. She knew that Neve was feeling the pressure of his big decision to move to the States, and she was the primary reason why.

<hr>

Gloomy gray skies opened up to blue by mid-afternoon as Jenae and Neve made it to the entrance of the Space Needle. They walked right up to the ticket booth with crossed arms in front of their bodies. It was chilly outside, but not as cold as the car ride over there. A sign read, "The Centerpiece of the World's Fair, April 21st, 1962."

"Oh look, this was built the year we were both born. It's 520 feet in the sky and is supposed to resemble a spaceship," Jenae said formally.

"Can we call a truce, so we can enjoy our trip again? I'm sorry that I paid too much attention to the hostess. I was pushing back on the marriage and kid thing because I didn't want you to win that argument."

"Oh really? Maybe you should sort out how you really feel. I'm not happy, but we can bury the hatchet for now."

Neve put his arm around Jenae's shoulder and pulled her into his body as they waited for the elevator to take them to the top of the tower. He kissed her on the top of her forehead, just where her hairline started. Jenae's body softened as her eyes filled with tears.

"I got you those pretty flowers."

"Oh, shut up. I know you bought them to give to Deely's wife for letting us stay at their place." Jenae couldn't hide her smirk.

"OK, if you don't want them . . ." Neve chuckled.

The vista from the top of the Space Needle was spectacular for city and water views; big cargo ships and ferries crossed the sound and seagulls flew in erratic patterns. The outline of Bainbridge Island was detectable, but the view of the mountains in the opposite direction was completely socked in with rain clouds. They were thankful for a little bit of sunshine. On the way out, they passed through the gift shop and Jenae stopped at the costume jewelry display. She touched a silver metal bangle with Space Needle charms.

"Look, this reminds me of the dolphin bracelet that was in my backpack. I thought it was from you because it was right next to the love letter that you wrote to me, saying that I was your reason for being, or something like that."

"I don't know that I said that, but I remember telling you nice things. I did not put that bracelet in there. It must have been from your secret admirer."

"The only person I can think of is Tim. You know we dated before you came to Hawaii. He drove me to the airport when I came back to the mainland. I'm the one that got away. I bet it was him, but we haven't talked at all since then. I'll have to figure out where he lives and give him a call."

"Now you are just being mean," Neve said.

"I do want it back from the detectives in Dallas. Maybe they'll send it to me."

"That bracelet is bad news. Remember, you were wearing it when that weird stalker found you at the hospital?"

They made it to the Deely abode exactly at 6 PM despite the stop and go traffic in down-pouring rain. Neve readjusted the flower stems to make the bouquet look fresh again.

"Welcome to Seattle!" Deely shook Neve's hand. "Good to see you again, man!"

"Thanks for having us. This is my girlfriend, Jenae."

Deely's wife greeted Jenae with a hug and quickly ushered them into the house out of the rain. Dinner with a bottle of red wine was waiting for them, and Neve's bouquet of fresh flowers sat in a vase in the middle of the table. Deely and Neve talked about New Zealand and airplanes mostly, while the women made small talk about college and sororities.

"I hope you have the morning free tomorrow, because I got special permission from the wing commander to take you both on an observation flight in my C-141. We have a practice mission in the area."

"Holy cow, that would be so cool. I thought you were just going to show me around the base and walk around some planes," Neve said.

"I've never done anything like that. Of course, we don't have anything better to do."

"OK, it's an early show-time, so we need to plan on leaving the house early to get to McChord by 6 AM."

The skies were clear for the early morning briefing. Jenae and Neve waited for the crew to finish and hung out in a stark waiting room with cement brick walls, linoleum tiles, and metal armchairs. After the walk around, Captain Deely escorted the pair to the grey C-141 transport plane with wooden chalks behind four-foot diameter tires. Deely welcomed them to the cockpit after climbing up the metal air stairs. With enthusiasm and expertise, he explained the panels of switches that made the airplane go. Neve listened intently while Jenae tried to keep from yawning. They found a seat on long red netting on the side of the plane with no windows.

"The two of you can alternate coming up to the cockpit. We only have one observer seat, so who wants to come up for takeoff?" Deely asked.

"You go ahead, Neve. This is your deal," Jenae said.

"This is great! Are you sure?" Neve reaffirmed.

"Absolutely. I'll see if sitting sideways is better than riding backwards," Jenae said.

Deely helped Jenae buckle into her spot for takeoff, and Neve waved and smiled as he walked to the cockpit.

"Clear for takeoff," Captain Deely said into the radio.

Chapter 10

Mount Tam

Jenae got a call from Sandy on Friday night after returning from Seattle with Neve. The trip ended better than it started because they both decided to put their egos and expectations aside while they had each other's undivided attention. Neve had set up a water plane ride on Saturday morning but there was only room for one passenger and Jenae didn't mind staying earthbound.

"How was your trip to Seattle? Did you get engaged?"

"Heavens no, almost the opposite. But everything is fine now."

"I was thinking of going up to Marin and checking out Mt. Tamalpais. Do you want to come hiking with me since Neve lives right there?"

"Sure. Maybe we can get dinner with him and his brother afterward."

"I want to hear all about Seattle on our hike."

The 8 AM show time at the trailhead turned into 9:30 because the ladies stopped for morning coffee and fresh bagels before taking on the great mountain's elevation of 2,579 feet. They each wore leggings and had light jackets tied around their waists. Sandy wore a small backpack with water bottles and trail mix inside, and a floppy hat to protect her fair skin from the piercing sun. Pine trees on the red dirt trail smelled refreshing, but the energy that they emitted created a relaxation only found in nature.

"My neighbor told me that mountain biking was birthed on this peak and the mountains all around here," Sandy said.

"Do you mountain bike? I tried once, and it almost killed me. I've known too many people who have fallen off a cliff or hit a tree stump and ended up with a punctured lung, or a broken leg," Jenae replied.

"I don't actually bike in the mountains, but it does sound cool. I'm shocked you don't. You're like a machine when it comes to exercise and adventure. Just look at your sports bra! It's so worn out that the elastic is popping out in the back. I'll buy you a new one if you need me to," Sandy said as she pulled on the frayed fabric and laughed.

"Maybe for Christmas. I like this bra; it's comfy. Hey, look up over the bay; I think that's a seaplane. Maybe it's Neve. It should be about the time that he's in the air."

The seaplane banked as it approached the summit of Mt. Tam and turned back to the bay. The ladies jumped up and down and waved their arms in the air, but there was no indication that the pilot or passenger saw them.

"I was hoping for a wing wave or something. How could they miss us? We are at the top of the peak," Sandy said.

"I'm sure we looked like little bugs to them. In Seattle, we went on an exploration flight with Neve's friend, Deely, who is in the Air Force. It was a huge gray plane, and he was on a mission to practice refueling and touch and gos at the base."

"Oh my gosh, that sounds crazy."

"For sure. So, I got to go up in the cockpit a couple of times during the touch and gos. It gave me perspective on just how small we are, and how much of the world I haven't experienced. The view from the cockpit is so different from passenger seats in the back."

"What's Neve's deal? I thought he was a real estate investor? Does he want to fly now?"

"He certainly is enamored with flying, and I'm pretty sure that's where his heart is now. I think it'd be cool for him to be a pilot. Just think, we could travel the world if he ended up on a commercial airline."

"Well, if he does and you are his wife, I want to go on a safari with you and your preteen son or daughter. I will bring mine; it will be a mom-teen double date."

"Sounds good, I'll mark it in my calendar. We better start heading down. Do you see the storm clouds building over the reservoir?"

"Where did everybody go? Are we the only hikers on the mountain now?"

"I have no idea which path to take back to our car, I wish we had a map."

The chatty pair gathered their snacks and empty water bottles and followed a streambed that led them to the other side of the mountain. Sandy told Jenae scary stories as they navigated tree trunks and loose rocks.

"Did you hear about the Mt. Tam serial killer? He was called the Trailside Killer. He murdered people on these trails."

"Are you kidding me? When was this?"

"Recent! Like ten years ago."

"Why would you bring me here? We are lost, a storm is moving in, it's getting dark, and a killer is probably following us, waiting for the perfect moment to attack."

"Oh, don't worry, we'll make it out as long as we keep going down in elevation. How hard could it be?" Sandy added.

As the sun dipped below the mountains to the west, Jenae and Sandy met a paved road that was nowhere near the trailhead where Sandy's car was parked. They walked for a mile until they found a pay phone at a gas station.

"I hope Neve is home to pick us up."

Neve was relieved to get the phone call; he had expected them to return hours before and darkness had settled in. Sandy was too tired to eat dinner and went back to the city to take a long, hot bath. Neve promised to drive Jenae back home the next day. After a grilled cheese sandwich, soup, and a hot shower, Jenae put on Neve's clean white t-shirt and threw her clothes in his washing machine while they watched Saturday Night Fights. He described the water plane landing on the bay with the excitement of a child. Jenae felt his joy but was still a little disappointed that he hadn't spotted them waving to him on the mountaintop.

<hr>

When they went to bed, Neve told her that Hamish had decided to leave the States.

"Why? Are you kidding me?"

"It isn't exactly working out for him as we planned. We have one more month on the lease in this apartment, and he isn't sure that he can stick it out any longer."

"That makes me sad. What does that mean for you? Are you leaving too?" Jenae panicked a little.

"I'm waiting for an extension on my visa. But if that doesn't come through soon, I may have to go back and reapply."

"What happens then?"

"While I'm waiting in New Zealand, I was thinking I could pick up another house to flip and start flying lessons. I really have a passion for aviation now that I've had all of these amazing experiences."

"What about the two of us?"

"I was hoping that maybe you could come out to Christchurch for about a month during your summer break from school. I would really like for you to meet my family and see where I come from. It would be winter there, but it doesn't get too cold because we're on an island. You would like it, I promise."

"OK, that makes me feel better. I would love to come visit you and see where little Neve grew up and went to school." Jenae leaned into Neve and gave him a soft kiss.

The night got emotional and intense. Both of them lay on their backs in the queen-sized bed and stared at the popcorn ceiling with a full moon casting a light through the vertical blinds. They held hands while tears dripped from the sides of Jenae's face. There was no sound except for one owl hooting in the trees and sniffles from Jenae's side of the bed.

"Come here. I promise you that everything will be all right. It's just going to be a winding road on our journey." Neve flipped Jenae on her side as he pulled into her. He looked into her eyes and wiped her tears, and she flung her leg over his and sunk into his chest. She felt protected and loved, but also uncertain that they would make it.

Their passion for each other quickly increased to a level of break up sex, or make up sex, or I may never see you again sex. Neve slid his hand under her t-shirt and rubbed her back. When the sexual tension reached its peak, he dramatically pulled it off over her head. He followed by pulling her head back by her ponytail and kissing her breasts as he gently cupped them in his hands. She only had cotton panties on as he slid his hand down to her bottom and between her legs. She leaned in and removed his loose shorts, and they were skin to skin for the rest of the night. Connected by love that neither could say out loud.

<hr>

The next morning, Jenae, Hamish, and Neve had breakfast together of tea and toast. Hamish acted relieved that he could get back to New Zealand because his business partners wanted him back and he could make good money again. He would miss the guys that he played with in the band and the camaraderie that he felt. Neve sensed defeat, and that Hamish would want to come back to the U.S. if given the opportunity.

Jenae gave Hamish a big hug at the car and wished him luck.

"See you this summer in your neck of the woods!" Jenae told Hamish.

"I hope not, because that means that Neve had to go back, too. But it'll be good to see you in any case."

Neve and Jenae hopped into the little red Ford Focus and puttered down the hill toward the highway. Marin County was a beautiful enclave, and Larkspur was a small town with no stoplights and an old-time movie theater with two movies shown every weekend. Neve pointed to the theater marquee that read, "Die Hard" and "Rain Man."

"I saw Danny Glover at the grocery store a few days ago; he must live around here," Neve said.

"Is he in one of those movies?" Jenae asked.

"Are you serious? We are going to the movies next week so that you know a little something about pop culture," Neve said.

"I am not a star-struck person. They're just people like we are," Jenae said.

"What about Robin Williams and Neil Young? I've seen them around, too. If I have to go back to New Zealand, I'm going to miss the specialness of this place. And you, too. But you'll be with me, so I won't miss you at all. We'll be together, right?"

"Right. Nice save. Hey, since I have my workout gear on, why don't you save some money and hassle and drop me off at the overlook parking lot at the bridge? I'll run home and get my workout in. I've walked on the Golden Gate, but I've always wanted to run across the whole thing."

"No, that's too much. I'll drive you home. You're afraid of bridges, remember?"

"I'm afraid of losing control in a car on a bridge. Really, I want to do this. I know my way back. It's a beautiful day."

Jenae kissed Neve goodbye and made her way to the bridge pedestrian sidewalk. She had to walk and slowly jog through tourists taking photos at the beginning, but quickly picked up speed as the crowd thinned out in the middle. She felt gentle wind gusts, but the warm sun kept the chill away. The bay looked vast and ominous, and the ocean side was choppy, with container ships cruising out to sea. The suspension bridge didn't scare her, but amazed her intellect. She didn't have an engineer's mind, but she did have an active curiosity about how this thing got built.

Running through the old Presidio Base was her favorite, especially as she rose on a shaded hill past the pet cemetery. It was a quiet, two-lane windy road with hardly any traffic. She cooled down as she walked the flat straight streets of the Marina District and stretched her hamstrings and calves on the mooring walls next to the boats.

She unlocked the front door of her shared apartment with Annie and found a note next to the phone. It said, "Check the answering machine. I'll be back on Monday."

Jenae listened to her only message from a Dallas Police detective. They had received her written and phone requests to return her bracelet in the investigation of the hospital incident. She should receive it by the end of the week. Jenae still wondered who gave it to her.

Chapter 11

Streets of San Francisco

Spring break seemed like a long distant memory once classes started back up, especially while Jenae worked two twelve-hour shifts on the cardiac unit at the big medical center. She spent her one day off in Marin County with Neve, but the chance of him getting a work visa without a legitimate marriage was next to impossible. She had called the immigration office, and even sat in the waiting room for hours with Neve, just to have the papers thrown back at her with no indication of what was missing from the document packet. His lease was ending at the beginning of the summer and his construction gigs had dried up. Jenae was very good at compartmentalizing, especially when it came to stressful situations; she had to. She was a nurse.

"Hey, who's my patient with the security guard outside of his room. Is the patient dangerous, or is someone after him?" Jenae asked the nurse going off nights in the shift report.

"I'm not sure, only that he's here for a cardiac catheterization and observation. The guard keeps asking me for cups of coffee, like I'm a damn waitress. I'm not his nurse."

"That's rude. Is the patient scary?" Jenae asked.

"No, he's actually really nice and normal. It's the security guy who's a huge asshole."

Jenae made rounds on her patients after gathering morning medications and organizing procedures. The patient with security was just as the previous nurse described. He seemed gentle and engaging while she restarted his IV and he didn't ask for anything from her. But the guard did.

"Hey lady, grab me a black cup of coffee, would ya?" the guard asked Jenae.

"There's a coffee pot in the canteen over there. You can check to see if anyone made a brew this morning," Jenae responded.

"Listen, I have to sit right here and make sure nothing happens to this witness and that means that I can't leave the door, even for a second. You'll have to get me a cup, I don't even want any cream or sugar. Just black."

Jenae raised her chin and planted her New Balance running shoes and was about to let the guard have it, when a tall professional man in a suit with a leather gun holster inside his jacket approached. The guard stood up and shook the government agent's hand and assured him that the patient/witness was safe and unharmed. The agent relieved the guard of his duties while he entered the room to interview the patient. The guard went to the canteen to start a fresh pot of coffee, use the bathroom, and visit the vending machines for a roll of tiny, powdered donuts. Jenae passed by the witness' room when the agent stepped out into the hallway.

"Is everything OK?" Jenae asked.

"Yeah, how long will this guy be in here?" the agent said.

"He has a procedure scheduled for late morning or early afternoon today, but the time could shift around. Depending on the findings, anything could happen; surgery, more monitoring, or he could be released. It's just a wait and see situation."

"OK, have you seen the guard? He has been gone a long time. I guess I'll have to wait here until he comes back."

"Can you tell me why the patient has security detail?"

"Sure. He's a witness in a big case coming up soon. It's a financial deal, and I doubt you'll see any bad guys, but this is a big deal for the prosecutor. He doesn't want to take any chances."

"What agency do you work for?"

"The FBI, I just moved up to San Fran from LA, partly because of this case."

"I ran into one of your agents while I was in Hawaii this summer. I think he lived in LA. Do you know a Logan? I don't know his last name. I saw it on a business card, but I can't remember it," Jenae said.

"Yeah, yeah. Logan relocated with me to San Francisco. He got here a few weeks before me; we're still learning the ropes together. What's your name again?"

"I'm Jenae. I think he had a little crush on me."

"Yep, that sounds like Logan."

The guard returned to his position with drinks and snacks, and the government agent waved goodbye to Jenae as he turned to walk away.

Twelve-hour shifts were a blessing and a curse. A nurse could get her hours for the week over a long weekend, but most days, she came to work in the dark and left in the dark. It was time she would never get back. A burrito truck across the street was Jenae's occasional salvation because she could walk outside and get fresh air and sunshine on her lunch break. Most nurses zipped through the cafeteria and grabbed a sandwich and ate it in record time so that they could retire to the "silent lounge," where nurses laid down on couches and took forty-five-minute naps before returning to the floor. Jenae took delight in watching the burrito maker scoop the chicken, rice, beans, cheese, and pico onto a steaming flour tortilla before folding it up just right so that nothing fell out. It reminded her of working in the mother-baby unit in San Antonio, and teaching the parents how to wrap their newborn babies up in the receiving blanket until they looked like a little burrito. The shift flew by, and at six o'clock, while patients were eating their dinner trays; she felt a tap on her shoulder. She jumped as she turned around. It was a guy about her height, or a little shorter, with a sandy crew cut dressed in a suit and tie.

"Hey, Jenae. Remember me?" Logan's eyes sparkled when he caught her attention.

"Logan? You look different dressed in a suit and strapped with a gun holster."

"My colleague said that he met you and that you mentioned that you knew me from Honolulu. I thought I'd come by and say 'hi' while I was in the neighborhood. It's kind of weird, huh?"

"Really weird. I just moved here from Dallas a few months ago, myself," Jenae said as she tugged on her scrub top, and lifted her chin.

"I remember you saying that you were from Texas when we had that beer at the beach restaurant in Waikiki," Logan said as he tilted his head and looked at Jenae with a twinkle in his eyes.

"Yep, I moved here because the guy that I met there moved here from New Zealand. You met him, didn't you?"

Logan adjusted the cuffs on his dress shirt and popped his neck back and forth as he looked past Jenae's face.

"So, he lives here now. What was his name? Neville or something like that?" Logan asked.

"Yeah Neville, but he goes by Neve. He's trying to make a go of it here, but he might have to go back to New Zealand for a while to reset his visa."

"I think we had a misunderstanding right before I left. He was probably just trying to protect you, but he was pretty aggressive with me. I think our egos got out of hand. I was mostly at fault."

"Emotions were high at that time, so I'm not surprised." Jenae was impressed that Logan owned up to his part.

"Are you living in the city? Let me guess, you are in the Sunset District? Definitely not in the Tenderloin. Hm, maybe the Marina or Pacific Heights?" Logan tapped his chin with his index finger.

"You got it, I'm living in the Marina right now," Jenae confirmed.

"I see. I'm closer to downtown, but I like to go jogging around the Marina because it's flat and next to the water. Can I have your number? Next time I'm down there, maybe we can get a cup of coffee and catch up?" Logan asked.

Jenae paused, and she heard her name called over the intercom for report. "Uh, OK. Sure, I guess."

She scribbled her number on the back of his card and gave it back to Logan. Logan reached his hand out.

"Here's a fresh card. Call me if you run into any troubles." Jenae slipped it into her top shirt pocket.

"OK, I've got to go. Talk to you later."

Logan thrust his chest out and got on the elevator with a knowing grin.

———— ◆ ————

A small brown box sat on a table near the front door of Jenae's apartment for nearly a week before she noticed it was addressed to her. She opened it and unwrapped the bracelet neatly packed in bubble wrap with an invoice rubber-banded around it. The note on the paper said, "Upon initial inspection, no tracking devices suspected. No further testing required. Return to rightful owner."

Hm, well that doesn't make me feel any better. It doesn't seem like they even checked it. Maybe it was from Tim, I should call Walker to get his number. Jenae thought.

Walker loaded the last plate from breakfast in the dishwasher when he heard the phone anchored on the kitchen wall ring.

"Hey Jenae, long time no see! It's good to hear from you. What's going on?" Walker said.

"I moved from Dallas to San Francisco, and I'm working and going to school here," Jenae said in a bubbly voice. She was tickled to talk to Walker after all he'd done for her in Hawaii last summer. He was a good and caring friend to her.

"Wow, that's a big change. You're showing off your smarts to the West Coast now, huh?" Walker said in his thickest Texas accent.

"Just trying to learn something new. What have you been up to? How's your brother Tim?" Jenae bounced her knee, and she leaned forward in her chair. The wound Tim caused by cheating on her last summer wasn't quite healed up.

"I'm just back in Houston living my best life. I'm working a construction job, and I have a nice, pretty, girlfriend."

"Good for you. Are you taking care of your mama, too?" Jenae asked.

"Sure am. Tim is helping me out with that. Well, he actually helps her out the most."

"So, I have a question to ask Tim about. Do you know anything about a bracelet in Hawaii?"

"No, can't say I do, but Tim will be really happy to hear from you, I can give you his number."

"Here, let me get a pen and paper to write it down. OK got it. Is he back in school, too? He took the GMAT to get into business school last summer, and as I recall, he got a really good score," Jenae said.

"Oh, hell no. Tim isn't in school; he's managing a strip club downtown. He got out of the Marines because he thought the grass was greener on the other side. He never got his legs under him again after he messed up y'all's relationship by cheating with Hannah. But he's good about taking care of mama."

"Classic! Well, that's good, I guess. Have you heard where Hannah is? You're still family friends with her mama, right?" Jenae asked.

"I'll be honest with you. Hannah came back to Houston too. At the beginning of the year, she and Tim hung out a few times. No matter how hard they try, their relationship just stays in the friend zone. I think she's in Northern California with Pami now. Y'all nurses move in packs, don't you?"

"Interesting. I haven't been in touch with Pami; I'll track her down. Let me give you my number in case I can't reach him so we can keep in touch. Send me a Christmas card! It's good to talk to you again, Walker. Take care."

"You too, Jenae. Bye."

The thought of talking to Tim again gave Jenae a sick feeling in her stomach. She placed the paper with his information next to Logan's in a box next to the telephone. The original traveling nurses ending up in close proximity in Northern California without even trying made Jenae pause. She still loved Pami and wanted to keep in touch, but both of them got preoccupied with serious relationships and lost track of one another. On the other hand, as far as Jenae was concerned, Hannah could eat shit and die for cheating with Tim behind her back.

Chapter 12

Hippy Dippy

Hamish made it back to New Zealand without overstaying his visa and managed to keep a few dollars in his bank account. He stepped right back into his role as a real estate broker and back-up bass player in his band. The journey to America wasn't a total loss, he had a few embellished stories to tell his mates about his few months on the northern hemisphere. Yoga kept his mind calm through the transitions. However, he did miss a meditation retreat that he had planned for Neve and him in the Mayacamas Mountains. It was already paid for and non-refundable, so Neve roped Jenae into going with him instead. She had learned Transcendental Meditation a few years before, but hadn't been practicing it like she should have. She had a gut feeling that Neve's time in the U.S. would be limited and Jenae focused on spending quality time with Neve while he was still there, so moving some shifts around at work was worth it to spend more time together.

Neve and Jenae rose early before the sun came up on Saturday morning to reach the retreat site for check in. After a two-plus hour drive, they were the last to arrive at camp, and they didn't look like any of the other participants. Jenae's pink athletic shorts were a bad wardrobe selection, and they stuck out like a sore thumb. Luckily for her, attention was diverted from her to Neve's athletic build, which brought disapproving looks from the buck-twenty males eating bowls of quinoa with sprouts and dandelions on top. They caught the tail-end of breakfast. Jenae tried the grain free bread because it looked the most palatable, but she ended up just having a cup of chamomile tea and was upset that she hadn't packed snacks. A class about proper calming yoga positions prior to meditation was covered, as well as the weekend schedule, which included three vegan meals a day and spending most of the time in isolation and silence while meditating three times a day. No electronics of any kind were allowed.

Jenae felt like her head would blow off after afternoon yoga and meditation. She had never tried to decompress to that degree and was woefully uncomfortable, and she was hungry.

"How much did Hamish pay for this retreat?" Jenae asked Neve.

"I'm not sure, but he's into this kind of stuff. He spent a year in India studying with a Yogi and ended up with terrible parasites."

"I'm sure we'll get something out of it; hopefully not parasites. All kidding aside, I'm too high-strung to drop down to this frequency so fast—it actually hurts," Jenae said.

"I don't do the yoga part every day, but the meditation feels really good to me," Neve said.

"What about the food? I'm used to just eating chicken and fish, but I've never gone full on vegan. It'd be OK if they just put a bowl of roasted nuts out, but I can't eat all the smelly raw stuff that I've never even seen before. I've never craved a hamburger more than now."

"I'll have to agree with you there. I tell you what, if the dinner that they serve tonight is inedible, we can sneak out of camp and try to find food somewhere else. There should be a town nearby."

"Deal." Jenae's mouth watered just thinking about it.

Between mediation sessions, participants were encouraged to take tree baths by walking through the forest in silence. They could hike with someone side by side, but talking was forbidden. Neve and Jenae sauntered down a path away from other humans and loud whispered to each other in a cheeky mocking tone.

"You know at the welcome meeting, did the Grand Poobah really say that we weren't supposed to have sex on this retreat?" Jenae asked, "Yeah, I think he did, and he was looking straight at us when he said it."

"Who else would he look at? Everyone else looked single and yes, I'm going to say it . . . stinky. I sure hope the showers work in these cabins."

"It may be a cold rinse, but I'm sure that's good for us, too."

The couple wandered off the trail with a blanket from the room over Neve's neck. The intention was to sit under massive redwood trees to commune with nature and breath in fresh air. They hadn't accounted for big trees blocking the sun and the breeze picking up to a whistling pace. Jenae's legs were covered in goose bumps; Neve rubbed them up and down trying to create enough friction to warm her. They tried to laugh quietly as they snuggled in the blanket, which was too small for the both of them.

"Shh, I think I hear the Grand Poobah coming!" Jenae kidded.

"Put your head under the blanket, and he won't see us," Neve whispered.

Their faces were cheek to cheek under the blanket with a red glow inside. It reminded Neve of the living room campouts that he had as a kid. Their noses were cold as they kissed and giggled. From the waist up, they were covered and in their own world, but their legs sticking out caught the attention of the Grand Poobah walking past. Neve felt a tap on his back. He lifted a corner of the blanket and peeked outside. "Yes?" he said.

"The two of you are making too big of a spectacle. Maybe you should head on back to your rooms and get some privacy there," The Grand Poobah whispered.

Jenae kept her head under the blanket and snickered in embarrassment.

After a shower and another meditation session, the pair put on warmer clothing and walked to the main cottage for dinner. They waited for the food to be presented and tried to have friendly conversations with others, but most were still in silence mode. They each placed a few scoops of healthy-looking food from the trays onto their plates and headed outside to eat on their own.

"I don't think this is going to hold me over until the morning," Jenae said.

"Let's just hang out here for a while, and then we can go back to our dingy cabin and make out or something until dark. I feel like a child sneaking around."

"It's kind of fun, like being at girl scout camp for me. We would sneak out of our tents and steal snacks while our leaders slept in their comfy beds. We were lucky to have a cot to lay our sleeping bags on."

"We didn't camp in New Zealand. It must be an American thing because we do have a lot of camper vans on the roads during the summer months. I assume they are all Americans touring the country."

Neve and Jenae pushed most of their organic vegan food selections into the trash bin, hoping nobody would notice. They smiled, waved and fast walked out of there. The cabin was chilly; the sun was setting and the time to escape to find real food in the black of night would come soon. Jenae had some serious questions for Neve in the meantime.

"Remember on your last night in Hawaii—you had words with the FBI agent at the bar? What happened exactly?"

"I told him to get the hell out and to leave you alone. He was clearly in to you. I would go so far to say that he was stalking you. It's a good thing he left the islands that night."

"What if I told you that I saw him again this week—at the hospital? His name is Logan, something or other."

Neve stoked his throat and paced to the door. He turned back to Jenae with a red face and said,

"I'm sorry—did you say that you saw that FBI dude Logan at your hospital? The guy who watched your apartment for two months on assignment and then another week after the mission was done? The asshole that watched us have sex in your bedroom through a telescopic lens from the apartment across the street? The same guy who was obsessed with you and followed you around Waikiki?"

"I don't know about him being obsessed with me. He might have had a little crush. He seemed nice and normal, and said that you two just had a battle of the egos—a misunderstanding."

"I can't believe it. How did he find you?"

"It's just coincidence, I guess. I had a patient under protection because he was supposed to testify in a big case, but then he had a heart attack. The FBI agent that came to check on him mentioned that he and Logan had relocated from LA. I guess Logan found out and came by before my shift ended. There was nothing I could do about it."

"Jenae, honey, you don't understand. I saw things in his spy nest that you didn't and don't want to see. He is not a nice guy; don't be so naïve."

"It was pretty evident that he didn't like you, either. He knew your name, Neville. Not Neve, Neville. He looked just as mad as you do now when I told him that you were living here."

"Stay away from him. I'm telling you, he's bad news."

"Well, his witness should be released from the hospital by the time I go back for another shift, so he won't be hanging around."

"But he knows where you work."

Jenae intentionally left the part out about giving Logan her home phone number in haste.

⚬

The mission to procure food at a nearby restaurant lost its gusto because of the uneasiness of their conversation about Logan. They snuck out of their cabin and quietly closed the doors of the car. As Neve turned the key to start the engine, Jenae dropped her head out of sight just below the steering wheel in case Grand Poobah was watching. Neve quietly navigated the dirt road with only a few crunches from crushed pine needles. The drive down a paved two-lane road toward town was quiet except for the staticky AM talk radio station that Jenae was able to find. It was a sports-talk show that she nor Neve knew nothing about, but it was something to fill the void of uncomfortable silence. They slowly drove past the only cafe in town, but the signage read that it closed an hour before their arrival, so they headed to the gas station to ask for suggestions.

"Hello, I was wondering if you can tell us where we can go to get a bite to eat for dinner?" Jenae asked the attendant.

"It's pretty late. Our greasy spoon closed a while ago, but there's a town about thirty miles that way. But come to think of it, by the time you'd get there, their restaurants would be shut down, too."

Jenae looked at Neve and hung her head as they both perused the snack rack.

"My favorite—Ding Dongs! I used to make special trips on my bike for these little chocolate cakes. We can get some Chex Mix, too and let's grab some Drumstick ice cream bars." Jenae's spirits were immediately lifted with sugar at her fingertips.

"I'll get this Pay Day bar, at least it has some peanuts in it, and I'll grab some drinks." Neve was less enthused with the selection.

Jenae paid for their snack dinner because she felt guilty for making a fuss about the healthy food at the retreat—and for giving Logan her phone number.

After a very unsatisfying dinner of junk food, they both lay awake in bed. Neve spooned Jenae from behind with one arm over her waist and the other underneath her neck.

Full body contact kept the shivers away underneath the thin blanket and worn-out comforter. They both breathed lightly, pretending to sleep. Jenae was wide awake because her stomach was in knots about Logan, and the processed foods made her nauseated, too. Neve couldn't sleep thinking about how he was going to tell Jenae about the tickets he booked to go back to New Zealand.

Chapter 13

Making it Nice

The extra bedroom in Neve's apartment in Marin County was empty since Hamish left the country. He invited Jenae to stay with him, and she was happy to spend every night with him even after classes and work. They visited the only coffee shop in town each morning before Jenae scooted down the highway across the Golden Gate Bridge to the city. She had faced her fear of losing control and careening off the side of the bridge. She wasn't panicked, but her palms still got sweaty until she reached solid ground.

Most of Neve's days included lifting weights at the gym and running the trails on Mount Tam. He had told Jenae that he'd probably be going back to Christchurch but didn't disclose that he actually had a ticket for a specific date next month. His heart was conflicted, and his mind was confused. He wanted to take care of Jenae, but also wanted to be true to himself. His multiple phone calls researching the timeline and cost of getting a pilot's license confirmed that he must return to New Zealand and get his ratings there. A class was scheduled to start a week after his planned return, and he received confirmation that he had been accepted into the program. It was less cumbersome and a lot more affordable, and he could work to pay for lessons and flight time. His long-term fantasy and goal would be to get his commercial license and be able to fly around the world, hopefully from America.

To ease the pain of his departure, he spent hours compiling his favorite songs that reminded him of Jenae and recorded them on a cassette mixed tape. He planned to wrap it up and give it to her for a "goodbye for now" gift when he left. He made two tapes. The extra one was for him to listen to on his Walkman on the sixteen-hour flight back home. Every morning, Jenae found a small note on the bathroom mirror, or kitchen counter or on the dashboard of her car. She always felt reassured her that Neve cared deeply for her.

"Good morning, Princess. Have a beautiful day and know that I'm thinking about you. XOXOXO Neve"

He was good at love bombing which raised a red flag initially for Jenae, but his personality was kind and easy and she had no more concerns.

◄O►

When the day came to announce Neve's departure date to Jenae, he sandwiched it between two pieces of good news. He sat Jenae down with a glass of wine after she returned from a long day at work and grabbed her feet and set them in his lap. As he pulled off her athletic sock and started rubbing her foot with lotion, he smiled and said,

"I got some really good news."

"Oh really? Did your visa get approved?"

"Well, not that good of news."

"I got accepted into the aviation program in New Zealand. So, I can start flying and work on accumulating hours for my license."

"Oh wow! That was fast. Congratulations! When do you start?"

"That's the thing, the program starts in three weeks. And I'm going to go back two weeks from tomorrow."

All the air rushed out of the room as Jenae pinched the skin at her throat and clutched a blanket that she grabbed from the back of the couch.

"It's so soon." She cleared her voice with watery eyes.

"I know, but I think this'll be good for us in the long run."

"We'll see. I hope I can carve out some time to see you this summer in New Zealand. Will you have time for me if I come out to visit?"

"Of course I will, silly. You may need to come with me to the airfield a few times to make sure I don't crash, but I'll show you all around my stomping ground. I'm excited for you to meet my mom and dad. Well, my dad is a little weird, but my sisters are nice and I'm sure they will all love you."

"It sounds like I'll have a lot of shopping to do for gifts for everyone. I know how this goes," Jenae said with an overwhelmed sigh.

"Don't worry about bringing anything for my family. They don't need a thing. But I do need you to make time for me one more time before I leave. I made a reservation at the Sonoma Wine Lodge for a couple of nights for a romantic getaway for the two of us. Will that work into your schedule?"

"Sure. I'll make it work. That sounds nice."

"If you're interested, we can go on glider rides, the vineyards are supposed to be quite the sight to see from a bird's eye view."

"You mean I'll be in a plane with no engine? Neve, I won't even go in a helicopter, why would I hop into a little cardboard airplane? I think I'll pass. You go on the glider, and I'll watch from the tasting room."

"You really don't mind? Maybe I'll do a discovery glider flight. It's more of an introduction to gliding and ground instruction."

"Knock yourself out. I might get a massage instead of tossing my cookies in a fishbowl at 3,000 feet."

⸻ ◆ ⸻

What started as a fun and innocent pleasure flight above the wine valley, turned into a full day gliding course with three aero-tows. Neve was excited to start the experience at daybreak, and Jenae was happy to sleep in at the local hotel on crisp, thousand-count threaded sheets, and six pillows supporting her body as she stretched into a starfish position on the king-sized bed. When he arrived at the airfield, Neve was paired with an instructor, who gave him a briefing before they headed out to the runway. The daylong program started with helping out with various tasks associated with gliding. He learned to keep a log of flying time, and he prepared to launch the glider each time he flew. Most flights lasted about thirty minutes, and he saw a different perspective each time they launched. His instructor had been to New Zealand for a gliding competition in Omarama, New Zealand, which was situated halfway between Christchurch and Invercargill. The Alps nearby created updrafts that allowed gliders to stay up for long rides, which made the tiny town a top overnight spot for visitors. The area also drew fishermen, hikers, skiers, artists, cyclists, and astronomers because it's remote beauty. Neve enjoyed talking to people about the beauty of his small country. Few could find it on a map, and an infinitesimal number had actually visited the island nation. His heart was feeling the tug and excitement of returning to his homeland and his family.

— ◆ —

"How was the flying? I guess I didn't realize that you'd be gone all day," Jenae said.

"Yeah, sorry. I didn't realize that it was such a comprehensive experience. I loved it, though."

"Well while you were gone, I got a massage at the spa and took a tour of a couple of wineries without you. But I got a few bottles of wine to share."

"Let's make this about us now. That was selfish to make today about me. What can I do to make it up to you?" Neve leaned in and kissed Jenae's neck. Jenae poured a glass of chilled chardonnay for Neve. "Hm, let me think about that." Jenae was tipsy from her wine tasting tours, which made her receptive to Neve's advances and randy for passion.

"You can start by taking off all of your clothes and joining me in our private hot tub on the patio."

Jenae had just showered and was wearing the hotel's white robe with the belt loosely tied around her waist, which gave Neve a peek-a-boo show of her teacup breasts and her bare thighs. Neve leaned in for another kiss and nuzzle and picked her up laughing and carried her to the hot pool. She held onto his neck as he dropped both of them into the warm water, clothes, and all. She wrapped her legs around his waist as he kissed her body. She pulled off his shirt over his head and flung it onto the terra cotta pavers. While singing a familiar stripper tune, *Ba bump, bump, bum.* Jenae twirled the belt ends and pulled Neve's face into her bosom as she shimmied and pulled him into her open robe. A gray-haired couple walked past on a sidewalk nearby and turned their heads toward them as the splashing in the hot tub became rhythmic.

Neve yelled out, "nothing to see here." Luckily, the dense shrubbery surrounding the patio blocked their view, and the couple smirked and looked at each other as if they had been in a similar situation in their younger days.

They drank wine and Jenae sat on Neve's lap. They talked about serious topics even though they had never shared the words, "I love you." The closest Neve came was that night when he told Jenae, "I can't see my life without you." It was good enough for Jenae; she was smitten and felt his seriousness in their relationship. They had more growing to do together before knowing if they could be together forever, especially because they came from different countries, but it still felt right.

Jenae was glowing at dinner that night in a shimmery pink slip dress and strappy high heels. She was rested after a post hot tub nap with Neve, and she felt validated and loved by her man, even though he was leaving the country soon. Having a long-distance boyfriend wasn't the worst thing in the world because Jenae was so busy with work and business school. Sometimes boyfriend time felt like having an extra part-time job even though it was fun and fulfilling. A six-week break away from each other would give them time to focus on their own ambitious achievements.

"Are you looking forward to seeing your sister's new baby?" Jenae asked.

"Yeah. When Hamish called yesterday to tell me she delivered, I was surprised because the baby came a few weeks earlier than expected. I kind of wanted to be there when she brought the wee girl home."

"This is the first grand baby for your parents? How exciting."

"I'm an uncle now, and it's a whole new era."

"I can tell you're thrilled. Have you thought anymore about having children of your own?"

"I don't think I'd be a very good parent. I have a lot of selfish tendencies, but I suppose it would depend, I think you would be an excellent mother. Are you sure you are set on wanting children?"

"Wow, I'm glad we've gotten around to this conversation before you leave. My position hasn't changed. Just like you can't picture the future without me, I can't see my life without having my own kids. Children are at the top of my priority list. This is a non-negotiable for me."

"I think we would have really good-looking children together. I just worry about when I'll be financially able to handle it. I need to provide for the family and right now, I can barely provide for myself."

"That's a valid concern, but I don't think anyone feels completely ready for children, yet they come anyway and somehow it all works out."

On the way back to Neve's apartment the next day, Jenae buried her head in a text book while Neve drove. She couldn't get the conversation about children to stop playing over and over in her mind.

Chapter 14

Making of a Bad Guy

Logan had a lot of friends and acquaintances in different government agencies, not just in the FBI. He'd met them at selective training sessions in Washington, D.C. and worked in collaboration with them on different cases in his ten years at the bureau. One friend in particular was a higher up at the Immigration and Naturalization Service (INS), and served as a gatekeeper for all resident aliens wanting to enter the U.S. on a permanent basis.

Logan hated the New Zealander, Neville, because he humiliated him in Honolulu over the summer in front of Jenae. It only added fuel to the fire, and Logan was determined more than ever to win Jenae over. In Logan's mind, Jenae needed him to keep her safe and they belonged together. He felt the chemistry they had together when they shared a beer at the restaurant that special night in Honolulu, and he still had the photos of her while the FBI was running surveillance for the bombing suspect. If anyone could protect her, he could. Thoughts of her tanned, fit, body wrapped in a towel after her showers ran through his mind. He knew that he would be able to satisfy her like he did in his erotic dreams every night. If only he could get her alone. He wondered if she liked the cute dolphin bracelet that he left for her in her backpack. *Sure, it had a tracker in it, but it's necessary to keep tabs on her to keep her from doing any stupid—like running off with that Kiwi asshole, Neve.*

Once Jenae reappeared back in his life in San Francisco, all systems were green for go. It was no accident that he got transferred there from L.A. just after Jenae arrived. He could monitor her location now that she had the bracelet back and knew she lived in the Marina neighborhood. *That lowlife druggie that I hired to keep tabs on her in Dallas went too far and blew his cover. He deserved to land in jail again. It's a good thing I flagged her ID when the hospitals in SF did background checks on her, otherwise I would've lost her forever,* Logan thought.

For as much desire as he had for Jenae, Logan had an equal level of hate for Neve. He used his government resources to identify Neve's immigration status and made it his mission to ensure that Neville would never be allowed to stay in the U.S. permanently. His buddy at the INS did a deep dive on Neve's visa file. The Bureau of Immigration didn't have any incriminating evidence that would preclude Neve from becoming a resident alien, or eventually a permanent resident of the U.S., especially if he married an American. Logan would find a way to keep him away from Jenae if it was the last thing that he did.

Logan was good at hiding his psychopathic ways; he learned techniques from his abusive father, who eventually committed suicide in the backyard of their three-bedroom white clapboard, home in Dayton, Ohio. Logan found his father's lifeless body hanging from a noose on a branch of the big mulberry tree one afternoon after he came home from school. He froze with mixed emotions before he shouted for his mother and ran for the phone to call an ambulance. The image of his father's sleeping face would pop into his mind frequently, but he felt normal when he could focus on a true love. He had a few other girls that he followed, but none as alluring as Jenae.

Logan had been engaged once, but his fiancée called the wedding off because he was controlling her in what she wore and ate. He treated his fiancée like a prize because she was cute, and petite, and desirable to most of his friends. He didn't want her to put on any extra weight and only wanted her to wear sexy short dresses with high heels. He liked her hair short and straight and his favorite colors on her were red and black; he hated her in green. When they were out for dinner, he smacked her ass in front of friends to show that she was his and he could do whatever he wanted. At first his fiancée was intrigued that a man loved her so much that he paid attention to the little details of her life, but after warnings from her friends and parents, she put the pieces together and figured out that he was a full-blown narcissist and only truly cared about himself. Childhood trauma does that.

Although Neve was disappointed that the U.S. government didn't live up to the expectation that he could get his visa extended after six months, he was excited to get back home to start flying lessons. He could get right into the program with a good month of bookwork before even seeing the inside of a plane. Neve loved reading, and learning and he was a good test taker. He was told that if he fully embraced the plan, and flew lots of hours, he could be qualified to fly multi-engine, wide-body aircraft in as little as eighteen months. The plan was to focus on his new passion in the air and create a fulfilling, prosperous career. The timing would work out almost perfectly with Jenae finishing her MBA just a few months ahead of that.

He couldn't believe that Jenae had made such a big deal about having children. She was still young at twenty-seven and had plenty of time to have babies. His sister was in her mid-thirties, and she had been married six years before she had her first child. He had heard of women starting families in their early forties. Jenae didn't agree with that math because she worked in OBGYN and learned first-hand about infertility and problems associated with geriatric pregnancies. Children were on the back burner in Neve's mind, but he did see it happening sometime in the future.

Jenae made reservations for Neve's going away dinner at an exclusive intimate cave restaurant. The dining area was dark and cool, and candles and fairy lights gave barely enough light to read the pricey food items on the menu. It was a good thing that Jenae had a credit card with a high enough limit to pay for a fancy dinner. She always ran low on funds and panicked a little every time the statement came in the mail. She needed a job that gave bonuses to get her out of debt purgatory. But for this night, she was willing to splurge.

Neve ordered an expensive steak with mashed potatoes and truffle sauce, and Jenae opted for a seafood pasta dish with a Caesar salad on the side. A bottle of red wine came to the table first, and the waiter had trouble opening it in the dark. Neve offered to do it by the candlelight and the waiter was embarrassed, but relieved. The cave felt cold, and a chilly conversation followed suit.

"I know that you're excited to start your flying journey, but I'm scared about what will happen to us when we're far apart again," Jenae said.

"It's not like I have a choice in the matter. I can't find enough work here to survive, let alone thrive and build a life for us."

"I know, but I would like to know that I'm a high priority in your life."

"You are definitely at the top of my priority list, but I need to chase my dreams, too. You are busy in school and working and I'll be doing the same, just on the other side of the earth."

"Oh, well, if you put it that way . . . it doesn't make me feel any better," Jenae said.

"I'm a pretty good letter writer. I think I was sending three posts a week to you at one point."

"Yeah, I really looked forward to those and seeing your handwriting. And the XOXO's at the end."

"When you come to visit in July, you'll get a better idea of where I come from. I can't wait for you to meet everybody. I'm extremely proud of you and all your accomplishments, and you're a loving, caring person. Any man would be lucky to have you; I'm just glad that it's me."

"Aw, you are so sweet. Thanks for reassuring me." Jenae leaned across the table and Neve leaned in and gave her a kiss in the candlelight.

"A toast to a wonderful dinner until we can do it again in New Zealand." Their wine glasses clinked in the darkness.

❦

While Jenae went to class, Neve packed up his things and gave his furniture away to the neighbor across the breezeway and left a lot of his belongings in the garbage containers in the parking lot of the apartment complex. He offered his peach couch to Jenae and helped her move it back to San Francisco into her apartment in the marina. It fit nicely in her big bedroom. Neve had never spent the night there, because her roommate, Annie, made it prohibitive to have any friends over. Annie was really unhappy to see that Jenae was moving back in and immediately slid a bill under her bedroom door for toilet paper and paper towels that Jenae would use in the next month. Paying over half the rent in a place she didn't stay wasn't enough. Neve offered to clean the toilet with Annie's toothbrush. On the night before Neve's flight, Jenae spent the night with him one last time, but this time in her own bedroom.

The evening flight seemed to come quicker than either Neve or Jenae expected. They ran some errands and then packed up his suitcases, loaded them into the trunk of the car, and headed to SFO airport. Once Neve checked his bags, they headed to a restaurant where they had a beer and a basket of sourdough bread and butter. Neve was anxious and excited at the same time. It was hard to tell which because it all felt the same to him.

"Shh, listen, I think they are calling your flight." Jenae perked her right ear up toward the ceiling.

Neve listened and looked at his ticket. "Oh shit, I think that's last call. I thought I had more time."

Both Jenae and Neve ran for his gate and the customer service woman smiled and said, "Are you Neville? We've been waiting for you. We are about to close the doors."

"Thanks for waiting for me." He looked at Jenae and gave her a hurried hug. "I'm going to miss you."

"I'm going to miss you, too. Have a safe flight." Jenae blew kisses to him as he turned to look back. Neve gave a wave and a sweet smile.

The hurried goodbye was a blessing for Jenae, like ripping a bandage off quickly. It was painful but not prolonged.

Chapter 15

Fade to Black

A middle seat on the Continental long haul flight to Sydney turned into a sideways good-sized bed because Neve had four seats to himself in his row. He tied himself in with one seatbelt, rolled up his jacket under his head, threw the thin blue blanket over his shoulders, and slept for seven hours straight. The bumpiness of the plane woke him as the flight entered a tropical inter-convergence zone where storms typically form over the equator. Neve had read about the phenomenon in an aviator magazine, and even though he was stuck vertical in his seat for a few hours because of it, he got to experience a little bit more of the dynamics of flying and appreciated the sturdiness of the aircraft.

He missed all the snacks and meals because of the turbulence and extended naps, so he was glad when the flight attendant tapped him on the shoulder to wake him up and threw a hot towel onto his lap for breakfast. A platter of yogurt, granola, croissant, and orange juice was carefully placed on the tray in front of him a few hours before landing. The coffee smelled nutty and delicious, and he need a few cups to keep him awake when he landed.

The overhead light lit small portions on the map of Sydney that Neve studied to get his bearings. It was dark the entire flight until time to land, and the sun shone brightly over the horizon. The pilots must have put on their aviator sunglasses while landing the Boeing beast. Neve wanted to look cool in aviators, just like Tom Cruise in Top Gun.

A flight through Sydney was his cheapest option and he used the opportunity to visit some college blokes who had set up temporary residence on a boat in Rushcutters Bay. Neve found a shuttle that dropped him near King Street; he planned to sightsee on his own until he met up with his blokes from *uni* later that evening. The walk down to Darling Harbor reminded him of his last, and only, holiday to Australia he had taken as sibling trip with Hamish and their sisters. His older sister got married shortly after. The pubs and restaurants hadn't changed much from what he remembered, and the views were still spectacular.

He hopped on a ferry and hung out on the open-air deck even though the breeze was a bit nippy. The tourist sweatshirt that he bought from a vendor with Chinese gear at the pier gave him a discount because the slogan was wrong. It said, "Wish you were beer," with a cartoon koala on the front. It was perfect for Neve, but it did get him thinking about Jenae again, so did the Sydney Harbor. It reminded him of San Francisco

Bay, although Sydney Harbor was more stunning with the Sydney Opera House as a beautiful beacon on the point.

On the ferry ride from dock to dock he drank a cup of hot tea from a small Styrofoam cup and watched pelicans diving for fish in the distance. The last stop on the boat ride was to the Sydney Zoo. As Neve walked up the tree-lined paths to the animal enclosures, he felt like a kid again. He loved animals and never went to zoos much as an adult; maybe he could visit as much as he wanted if he had a couple of children. *I could get a family pass every year and see the wonderment again through my children's eyes,* Neve thought. His favorite animal was the Red Panda.

———◆———

His buddy's boat was docked in a marina further down the harbor and the cab ride over wasn't as expensive as Neve thought it would be. They were expecting him after 5 PM, and he arrived just after 5:15 PM with two cartons of beer, one in each hand, and a full traveling pack on his back. He had checked his larger bags into a locker at the airport until he left for Auckland the next day.

A grill with meat smoking on the outdoor deck of the boat was manned by his best buddy from university whom he hadn't seen in years. Hamish had been in touch and set up the visit between the old school friends.

"Hey Neville! It's been a long time since we've seen you, mate! It's good to see you man."

"Yeah, too long. Neither of you has changed a bit. You still look like the nineteen-year-old wankers trying to memorize anatomy," Neve said.

"Your smooth talk hasn't changed either. It's a miracle we all passed that class. That was a long time ago. What happened to you? You were gung-ho on becoming a foot doctor or something. I remember you were dating that girl at uni pretty seriously and then you broke up and left town."

"That was seven years ago. I guess I should have kept in touch. But I'm glad Hamish has been in contact. I joined the police force and was a cop for most of that time."

"That sounds cool. Did you see much action?"

"Yeah, a little bit. What about you guys? I heard you both joined the Army and now you're sailing around the Tasman Sea? Is the "ditch" as treacherous as has been reported?" Neve asked.

"Ah, nah. Sailing is pretty tame between New Zealand and Australia as long as you know what you're doing."

"University wasn't in the cards for either of us, so we made friends with some Army guys at the recruitment fair and signed up on a whim. We got paid to play war and hang out with some upstanding blokes. We didn't get deployed much."

"What are you doing now?" Neve asked.

"We both served our time and got out. Neither of us has a serious girlfriend or anything right now, and I'm trying to figure out what's next. My grandpa left me this boat when he died last summer, and I just wanted to take a break and enjoy life before anything got serious again."

"Sorry about your loss, mate. But that's cool that you have a piece of your grandpa's joy. Thanks for letting me stay on the boat tonight." Neve passed out beers to his old friends. "A toast to Captain Grandpa, may he keep your seas calm and your adventures exciting."

"Hamish said that you were living in America. Now you're back? How was it?"

"I'm not going to lie; it was the hardest slog of my life. I couldn't gain any traction for making money. It's illegal to work without a permit, and the under the table construction stuff was tough; it dried up pretty quick."

"I heard there's a girl you are pretty keen on."

"Jenae, yeah. She's a really special girl. We met in Hawaii last summer. My friend from the police academy and I went on a two-month holiday to the States and I met her at the tail end of that trip. She picked up her life and moved it to San Francisco for me mainly, so I feel bad that I had to come back to New Zealand and leave her there."

"Bloody Hell! If I'd done that, my head would've been on a stake."

"I know, it's pretty bad, but she's coming out to visit in July and maybe I can convince her to move to New Zealand."

"You're going to need a sparkly ring to convince her of that."

Heavy gray fog rolled into the bay as Jenae started out on her late afternoon run down Scott Street to the Marina Green. Foghorns from container ships blew loud and low but were ghost ships as they approached; they were impossible to see from shore. On her second turn around the path, Jenae closed her eyes and let out a sigh that was a mixture of hope and sadness. When her eyes opened, she saw a figure in the distance seated on a park bench tying his shoelaces. He had a black baseball hat on with orange SF Giants logo on the front. As she approached in a slow jog, he turned his head toward her and smiled.

"Hi, Jenae. I knew I would see you here eventually."

"Oh, hi Logan." Jenae startled while she glanced around without really seeing anything. "What are you doing here?"

"I'm just here to get a run in after work. I think I told you that I like to unwind with a good run along the water. How've you been?"

"I could be better. My boyfriend, Neve, went back to New Zealand the other day and I'm working a lot."

"Last time I saw you, I think you were expecting for him to get his visa extended. Did he run into some troubles with that?"

"Yeah, no it didn't get the extension after all, even after I spent an entire morning waiting in immigration with him. They were no help at all."

"The waiting room at the immigration office downtown is brutal. I had to go one time with a friend of mine. I feel your pain," Logan said.

"Hey, do you have any contacts in immigration that could help us out? I'm sure you know a lot of government employees."

"I would do anything to help you, Jenae. Let me ask around and see if I can figure anything out."

"Oh, that would be wonderful! I'd be so appreciative if you could help us."

"Here, take one of my cards again, just in case you lost the last one. Call me if you need anything."

Logan walked away, satisfied that his interference had been effective. A smile washed over his face as he puffed out his chest once his back was to Jenae.

⸺◦○◦⸺

"What the hell is happening?" Annie called Jenae on the phone at the hospital just after morning report.

"What do you mean? Are you OK? What's all the commotion in the background?" Jenae blinked rapidly as she touched the base of her neck.

"A bunch of police and SWAT are here. They busted down the front door looking for a kidnapper!" Annie said.

"What did you say?"

"Cops are swarming everywhere!"

"Everything was quiet when I went to work this morning. Was someone kidnapped?" Jenae asked.

"NO! But they thought so because someone called to report a kidnapping at our address." Annie cried hysterically.

"Can you call someone to get you out of there? I can't really leave my shift right now. But everyone is all right as far as you know right?"

"I don't know what to do, Jenae," Annie whimpered.

"Hey, there is a business card in the box next to the phone with the name Logan something or other on it. He's an FBI agent. Can you find it?"

"Yeah, I see it. I have it."

"Call him and tell him you're my roommate. He'll know what to do. I'll check on you a little bit later. I'm being paged for a patient, I gotta go."

<hr>

When Jenae returned to the apartment later that evening, the front door was secured with a large piece of plywood nailed to the frame. She entered the apartment through the garage. Annie's voice was shaky, and she paced back and forth as she told the story to the landlord on the phone. Jenae sat down on the chair across from Annie with a solemn look on her face. She sat quietly with her hands folded while she waited for the telephone conversation to end.

"Are you OK?" Jenae asked.

"No, I'm not OK. Our apartment was invaded by a dozen militant men with big guns. They pointed them at me, and screamed at me to get down on the ground. I'm fucking scared and traumatized. How could this happen?"

"Was it a fake call? Why would anyone call in a false kidnapping?" Jenae asked.

"I don't know, but I can't live here anymore. I told the landlord that I'm moving out as soon as possible. I don't feel safe here anymore." Annie broke into tears.

"I'm sorry. This sucks big time. Did you get ahold of Logan, the FBI guy?"

"My call went straight to an answering machine. He hasn't called back yet."

Jenae grabbed the broom and swept up debris from the entryway. "Can I pour you a glass of wine? I know I could use one."

Chapter 16

New Digs and Santa Cruz

A stop at the student information board in a hallway of the administration building at the university proved fruitful. As Jenae pulled tabs off advertisements for roommates that were stapled to cork board; Paulina walked up with her own poster and stapler in hand with a big smile on her face.

"Hey," Paulina said.

"Hey, how are you?" Jenae replied.

"Excuse me, can I put this up? I need to rearrange some of these other posters so I can make room for mine."

"Sure, do you want me to hold something?" Jenae offered.

"Do you mind grabbing these as I take them down?" Paulina handed Jenae old duplicate posters as she repositioned her advertisement for a room to rent in her two-bedroom apartment.

"Are you a student here?" Jenae asked.

"No, probably technically I'm not supposed to be using this, but I have a cool two-bedroom apartment nearby and my roommate moved out last week. My parents said they weren't helping with rent anymore, so I need to find someone to fill it fast."

"Where's your apartment?" Jenae asked.

"It's virtually down the street from the university, like a half block away. Are you looking for a place to live?"

"Yeah, I live at the Marina for now, but I want to find a place close to school. I'm an MBA student here. I also work as a nurse at the medical center across the park."

"Oh sweet! Do you want to live with me? I can show you the apartment right now if you have time."

"OK, sure. Let's go have a look."

Paulina was an intern for a graphic design firm downtown and her father, Dr. Paul and her mom lived south of the city on the ocean. It was Paulina's childhood home. The apartment on the second floor was bright and clean. Jenae would occupy the smaller second bedroom and use the hallway bathroom with a skylight above the toilet. On the walk up the stairs, they ran into a third-floor neighbor. Joe was tall, dark, and handsome with a gap between his front teeth and had worked for Kohler toilets in Wisconsin. He was also an MBA student and tried his best to convince Jenae that she should move in. He could vouch for Paulina, even though she was a little hippy-ish, having just graduated from the University of Colorado.

"Are you a first year or second year?" Joe asked.

"I've been here one semester, but I haven't seen you around," Jenae said.

"We're in different classes because I'm a second year. If you need any suggestions on professors to take, just holler at me. I still have three more sessions to finish up, so I'll be here through the fall."

"Yeah, thanks. I should finish by next year. I started my MBA in Dallas and transferred."

"You know what the best part of this location is?" Joe posited.

"No what?" Jenae's eyes opened wide.

"There are public tennis courts right next door. Do you play tennis?"

"I did in high school, but I'm terrible at it."

"OK, well that's not the best part then. The best part is that the university's new rec-center is right there on the corner, right across from this apartment building. You look like you work out—do you like to work out?" Joe asked.

"Sure do. OK, you sold me on it, Joe. When can I move in, Paulina?"

"I know it was my good looks." Joe laughed and waved as he walked away.

"He must have sold a lot of toilets. What a good salesman!" Jenae said.

"Hopefully he won't ask for a commission," Paulina said.

⚬

Sandy invited Jenae for a day trip to Santa Cruz to hang out on the beach and to check out carnival rides on the boardwalk. One of her fleeting boyfriends from college was a big beach volleyball star, and he was playing in a tournament there. Jenae's friend, Pami, from Hawaii, whom had recently relocated to the South Bay, agreed to go with them. Sandy drove the girls in her pristinely clean, leased BMW. After picking up Pami in Sunnyvale, they drove through the Santa Cruz Mountains to the ocean. The drive would have been relaxing, except for the constant chatter, giggles, and restrained screams from the ladies talking about their latest dates.

"I have to tell you about my date last weekend." Sandy started in her deep sexy gravelly voice. "So, I've been dating this guy for a couple of months; it was fairly steady but not too serious. We met two of my couple friends for dinner at a nice restaurant in the city. It had just opened, and reservations were hard to get, so of course I had to go. At the end of a fabulous dinner, the waiter split the check three ways between the couples. It was a normal, fancy dinner with a couple of bottles of wine, so it was a little bit expensive. But when the waiter handed my date the check, he looked at it and handed it to me and said, 'since they're your friends, you're paying.' I was flabbergasted. What do you mean they're my friends therefore I was paying for dinner? So I pulled out my credit card and put it on the bill with the others, and as I did, I saw my friend across the table whispering into her husband's ear, 'We'll never see him again.' So, he takes me home, and I said 'goodnight' at the front door and it was clear he wasn't coming in. And he's all like, 'Are you really mad at me for not picking up the check?' I told him that he embarrassed me in front of my closest friends. And he was like, 'but this is the first mistake that I've made in our relationship. My final words to him were, 'and the last one. Goodnight.'"

"And there it is . . . the reason why Sandy's the baddest bitch in the Bay! I love it," Jenae said.

"I thought you dated Jenae's brother. Isn't that how you know each other?" Pami asked.

"Well, he and I were steady until he broke up with me at that restaurant in Palo Alto. He said, 'Sandy, I have determined that you are not the woman that I will marry.' I was furious. He had no good reason, just that we were getting too serious. Whatever," Sandy said.

"What made him think that you would agree to marry him, anyway? Sounds like a wanker move. Didn't you have your sights set on Bill Gates for a while?" Jenae asked Sandy.

"I know what a wanker is, but who's Bill Gates?" Pami asked.

"He's the founder of a software company, Microsoft. You wouldn't know him unless you were in the tech industry like I am."

"Well, is it true?" Jenae asked.

"I had only met him in a social setting one time, but I did corner him in a parking lot early one morning to try to sell him some software. He freaked out a little and turned me down.

He's a nervous, antsy guy. I probably couldn't fake interest in him even for one date."

After they parked on an open sand lot, they unloaded the trunk of the BMW, and carried beach chairs, towels and a big cooler full of drink and snacks to a sunny spot in the sand, not too close to the crashing waves, and close enough to see the players on the volleyball courts.

"I can't wait to check out the boardwalk," Pami said.

The volleyball tournament was smaller than Sandy expected, but she got to give her ex a big hug and catch up with him again. She was a good friend with his sister who lived in San Francisco too. "It's funny; I come out of broken relationships with really good friendships with the sisters."

"I hope we are life-long friends, Sandy," Jenae said.

"Me too."

⸻◆⸻

As the women walked to the boardwalk, Sandy inquired about the police swatting that took place at Jenae's apartment. She was extra concerned because Sandy was the one who connected Jenae with Annie when Jenae moved to the Bay Area. Annie was extremely upset.

"I can't believe the cops broke down your door and thought someone was being held hostage!" Sandy said.

"Wait, what? What happened?" Pami was clueless.

Jenae reenacted the scenario with Annie on the phone and the aftermath when she got home.

"I don't know, Sandy. Is Annie involved in something illegal or dangerous? I never really saw her much until Neve moved back to New Zealand. And she was never really friendly with me. She was bossy, to be honest," Jenae said.

"Have you met Neve, Sandy? Don't you just love his accent? I'm taking full credit for introducing them in Hawaii last summer," Pami chimed in.

"I do like Neve a lot, but . . . and it's a big but, just because you fell in love with his accent, it doesn't take away the huge ocean that separates you. How in the hell are you going to make this relationship work with him on another freaking hemisphere?" Sandy said.

"Good point. And it doesn't sound like he's getting a visa extension anytime soon," Pami added.

"I have one thing up my sleeve. There's this guy who's in the FBI who knows some people in Immigration, and he said that he would look into it for me," Jenae blurted out with instant regret because she realized that Pami knew him too, from when he surveilled their condo over the summer. "I ran into him a couple of times since I've been here. Once at the hospital and again just the other day while I was out jogging."

"How do you know so many Feds?" Pami asked. "He doesn't have anything to do with the surveillance last summer, does he?" Pami asked.

"Well, as a matter of fact, it's that guy Logan from last summer." Jenae braced for impact.

Pami's face turned red, and she planted her feet wide in the sand when she stopped walking and turned to Jenae in a jerk. "Do you mean Logan, the guy who followed you and tried to date you and had a fight with Neve at the bar the night before he left the island, Logan?"

"Yep, that's the one. He moved to San Francisco not too long ago and our paths keep crossing," Jenae said.

"And you think he's going to help get Neve back into the country?" Pami said.

"It's my best shot. I don't mean to defend him, but we may have misjudged his intentions. He seems really nice and willing to help." Jenae said.

"Well, you know how I feel about him, Jenae. 'Stay away' would be my advice," Pami said.

The ladies dropped the subject of men and dropped their stomachs behind on each downhill run on the rollercoaster. But nothing compared to the tower drop, which left their hair standing on end and Jenae with a slight case of laryngitis. She sounded more like Sexy Sandy after that. Pami and Sandy rode on the pirate ship that swung with nauseating severity—back and forth, back and forth further until the ship swung all the way over as the riders hung upside down over the shore. Jenae would have completely lost her voice on that beast.

⸺◆⸺

The arcades were a lot less alluring after the traumatic excitement of almost dying seventy feet in the air. The sandy-footed girls packed up, loaded the trunk of the BMW and headed back over the mountains toward the metropolis.

"Did you know that we are driving over the San Andreas Fault right now? I just read an article about it, and it runs from here all the way north through San Francisco and up to almost Eureka, way up north. And it runs all the way south to about Palm Springs. Apparently, the fault is the boundary between the Pacific Plate and the North American Plate. It slices California in two. San Diego, Los Angeles, and Big Sur are on the Pacific Plate, and San Francisco, Sacramento, and the Sierra Nevada are on the North American Plate," Pami said.

"Good to know. I wonder what would happen to places like the Marina if a big earthquake hit. My place is built on a big patch of reclaimed land. I wonder if it would just melt the neighborhood into the bay. It would probably be safer to live on solid rock," Sandy said.

"I'm moving to solid ground soon. If anybody wants to build muscle, I'm going to be moving into a new place next to the university in a few days. Annie has already moved out to her friend's couch until she can find something else. The SWAT really scared her."

"I thought I knew her pretty well, but I think she may have some psychological issues now that I think about it. And no, I don't want to build muscle, but I'll bring over a nice housewarming gift!" Sandy said.

<hr>

When Jenae got home, she called Logan, and he picked up. He was working late hours in the office and was willing to help her move her possessions to her new, safe apartment on Lone Mountain.

Chapter 17

Moving Day

Logan showed up five minutes early to the broken-down door of Jenae's apartment. He knocked on the plywood board that was nailed in place.

"Hello! Is anybody in there?" Jenae peeked around the building from the garage. She looked up the outdoor stairs at Logan. "Hi! You'll have to come around back. Thanks for showing up to help me move. It's a good thing you have a pickup truck too, it saves me on renting a moving van."

"Sure, no problem. I had some free time this morning and I'm happy to spend it with you, even if it means breaking a sweat moving couches and boxes."

"I probably could do it myself, minus the bed and couch. I appreciate that you'd help me with this."

The truck bed was just large enough to accommodate the peach couch, bed mattress, and a few boxes. The rest fit in the back of Jenae's Camry. She gave Logan the address of her new apartment just in case she lost him at a red light. She didn't know that he was an expert at following people.

When he arrived at Jenae's new digs, Logan parked the truck on the curb just outside of the small apartment building. Jenae stood at the front door waiting for Paulina to buzz her in. It took a few tries to rouse her new roommate from sleeping off a hard night of partying.

"Good morning, Paulina. This is Jenae and my moving crew. Can you buzz me in?"

"Oh, yeah. Sure, I almost forgot that you were coming today," Paulina said. BUZZ, BUZZ, BUZZ.

"OK, I got the door open," Jenae said.

"Give me a second to get dressed and I'll meet you at the top of the stairs," Paulina said through the speaker.

Jenae propped the front door open with a big stone that was sitting next to the building. Logan pulled the boxes from the truck and placed them on the sidewalk.

"Should we take the big items up first?" Logan asked.

"Let's just grab some small boxes and get the lay of the apartment. I'm almost positive Paulina said her old roommate took their couch, so mine should slide right into that spot."

Paulina greeted the moving duo in a t-shirt, sweatpants, and no bra. Her hair was mussed, and she squinted her eyes. "Come on in, don't mind me, I had a late night. Too much Jägermeister, I guess."

She showed Jenae her room and pointed to the area along the long wall in the living room where the couch would fit. A couple of cabinets in the kitchen were cleared out and a shelf in the refrigerator was designated for Jenae. It warmed

Jenae's heart that her new roommate thought ahead for her belongings. Paulina filled a cheap blue plastic cup with ice and tap water and found the extra keys to the apartment in a drawer in the kitchen.

"Here are your keys. Make yourself at home, because this is your home now. Nice to meet you . . ."

"Sorry, I didn't introduce you. This is Logan," Jenae said.

"Oh, I assumed you were Neve. Sounds good. Sorry, but I'm going back to bed now. The room is spinning, and I'm nauseated." Paulina held on to the walls as she gingerly made her way back to her bedroom and gently closed the door.

The amateur movers made short work of the boxes and furniture. All of Jenae's belongings were inside the apartment in less than thirty minutes.

"I'll put my bed together later, we can just leave the boxes in my closet and bedroom."

"I wish I had more time to help you get situated," Logan said.

"Oh no, no. You've done more than enough. Thanks for helping me this morning. Can I buy you breakfast? There's a bakery over on Geary, not too far away," Jenae offered.

"OK sure. Should we both drive? I have about an hour before I need to be somewhere," Logan said.

"Follow me."

They both ordered coffee. Logan got a small quiche and Jenae picked out a pastry and asked for it to be heated. Logan insisted on paying, even though it made Jenae self-conscious.

She knew that neither Neve, nor Pami, would be happy with her decision to be near Logan, but she needed help and wanted to debrief with him about the swatting.

"Do you want to try a bite of my quiche? It's really good, here I can cut off a chunk," Logan said as he held up a bite-sized piece on his fork.

"No thank you. I'm really allergic to eggs, especially like that. It sends me into a weird immune response that can put me down for days."

"That's weird, and scary. So, what happened with the kidnapping deal? Your roommate left a message at the office that day, but I was out of town on a case. I feel so bad that I wasn't able to help you."

"That's OK. Fortunately, I was already at work when the cops busted down the door. But Annie is severely traumatized and wanted to move out, so I decided to move too since I wasn't officially on the lease. I hope she'll be OK. We still don't know how it all happened.

"I don't know what to tell you, maybe someone was trying to scare you or get back at Annie for something," Logan opined.

"Our only option is to move forward, I guess. It might be a little sporty living with a twenty-two-year-old pothead, but I don't plan on being home much. I'm so busy. And Paulina has really funny stories. She told me that her dad, Dr. Paul, was set up on a date with the politician lady, Diane Feinstein, when they were young. He is a prominent doctor in town and his last name sounds Jewish. Turns out he isn't Jewish, and they only went on one date."

"I wish I had a roommate, or a girlfriend, or both. A wife would be even better," Logan said.

"So, you've never married?" Jenae asked.

"I was engaged once, but it didn't work out. I guess the stressors of my job didn't help my situation. How about you?"

"I've never been married or engaged. But I did live with a guy in Texas, and he wanted to get married. I didn't. In Texas, I was told that if you live together and then declare in public that you are married, then you were legally married. So, this guy that I let live with me, for mostly health reasons, would try to do that. We'd go out after work to get dinner with a group of friends and each time he would toast to he and I being married. I would interrupt each time and deny it," Jenae said.

"Where's he now? Did he ever get married?"

"I doubt it. The last I heard, he is back in England with his mom. He still owes me 600 bucks for paying his bills," Jenae said.

"I hate to cut breakfast short, but I better get going. I'd like to continue our conversation. I've got tickets to the musical Les Miserable tomorrow night; do want to use them with me? Otherwise, they'll go to waste, my date had an out-of-town emergency."

"Ah, well, hmm. It's not a date; I can go just as friends. And I'll meet you at the theater, no dinner or anything," Jenae said guiltily.

"Yeah, sure! I know you are involved with your New Zealand guy. In fact, I'll check again with my immigration friend and see what he found out today. I'll fill you in on the details."

"Sounds good. I'll see you tomorrow night."

"I've gotta go. See you then."

"Bye."

Jenae felt proud of herself for getting moved in so efficiently, and now she had this guy working on Neve's immigration case. *What's everybody so worried about with this guy? I mean, sure he likes me and probably wants to date me, but I've been in stickier situations.*

The rest of the day would be devoted to unpacking, but Jenae didn't want to disturb Paulina's sleep anymore, so she wandered over to the new workout center with her bathing suit and goggles in hand. She had heard about their state-of-the-art natatorium but also wanted to check out dance classes for fun and the exercise machines.

She was stoked that the massive gymnasium was included in her student fees. The pool temperature was warm, almost too warm to swim laps at any level of intensity. She watched a group of white-haired ladies in the corner jumping up and down and lifting their arms with buoy dumb bells. Music from the seventy's echoed against the walls in the hollow structure, but the water-aerobic mermaids followed the tune, and caught each beat with the instructor standing on the deck trying her best to show them moves while balancing on one leg.

A teenaged boy, with obvious physical handicaps, hung in mid-air on a hydraulic lift as a swim teacher maneuvered him into the pool next to a broad cascade of steps. His face lit up, and his smile turned to an O shape with eyes widened as two instructors guided him into the warm waters below. Jenae cut her workout short and headed for the sauna and showers in the spa-like locker room. She picked up a flier from a table that highlighted class schedules and then headed to the weight room for a look around.

Jenae felt comfortable in the room full of machines because she had learned weight training in high school as part of the swim team. On weight training days, she arose at 5 AM to take a shower, dry her hair, and put hot curlers in before heading to the school gym in the morning darkness. After parking in a primo space, she would pull the clips off each cooled roller and drop them in the passenger seat beside her. Her curls cured in place during her workout, as she pulled down on bars and lifted weights above her chest. At the end of the session she took another quick body shower in the school locker room and combed out her wavy hair.

Two classmates from the MBA program were socializing amongst the bell bars; she was happy to join in and catch up on the latest gossip going around the university. All three of them eventually made it to the very top of the building to a cute sandwich shop for lunch. Jenae ordered a turkey submarine sandwich with extra banana peppers. It was a large potion for the price. They chatted about classes and her new roommate as they sat at a table overlooking her new apartment building; the sky was clear and blue.

After her friends left, Jenae realized that she still had postcards in her backpack that were beckoning her attention. Out of guilt she started to write them both at the same time to Neve. She had fallen behind and wanted to catch up to make sure he felt loved. Plus, she wouldn't have to describe the non-date that she was about to go on with Logan.

⋅◦⋅

Les Miz started at 7:20 PM, and Jenae ducked out of class thirty minutes early to make it to the venue downtown before the stage lights went down. She met Logan in the entry area near the door. He had her ticket and handed it to the greeter for her to enter the theater.

"I'm glad you could make it. This show's supposed to be amazing. Come on, we're in Orchestra seating. We only have a couple of minutes to get in our seats," Logan said.

"Sorry about that. I should've allotted more time to get over here." They quick stepped down large red-carpeted stairs to the second door from the stage. Jenae wore a black leather mini-skirt with a white t-shirt under a long silky-pink jacket.

"Excuse me. Sorry, thank you," Logan said to the fancily dressed patrons in sequins and black suits as he and Jenae stepped over their shined, leather wing tips and pumps.

"Ah, we made it just in time," Logan whispered.

Jenae self-consciously tugged on her skirt to cover her thighs when she sat down, and noticed Logan's polished Florsheim shoes with red aglets on the end of the laces.

"What's the story with your laces? Are colored aglets in style now? Jenae asked.

"I picked them out at a specialty store to show my colors for my alma mater. I like weird things like that," Logan said.

"Interesting. So, I remember trying to read this novel in high school French class, and all I remember is that Jean Valjean was poor and thrown in prison for stealing a loaf of bread for his starving sister. And that a horrible police inspector had a vendetta against him and wouldn't stop pursuing him," Jenae whispered back.

"That led into the revolutionary period in France, where young idealists tried to overthrow the government in Paris," Logan said.

Lights from the stage shone on their faces as the curtains opened for the first act. The scenes were dark and scary and swelled feelings of sadness in Jenae's belly and love in her heart at the same time. The beautiful music made her confused and emotionally overwhelmed. Tears that welled in her eyes streamed down her cheeks and she couldn't get them to stop, and she didn't have any tissues, so she swiped the tears away with her index finger like a windshield wiper on a car. She had no idea that she'd react with such volatility. The sadness that she felt surprised her, and she was embarrassed, especially with basically a stranger next to her.

The finale of the musical only led to Jenae trying desperately to hold in a wailing cry. She tried to think of stupid funny things that would stop her from cry-heaving and wailing in public. She looked up and away from the stage and took slow, deep breaths, but it didn't help. It was one of the most embarrassing moments of her life. Her eyes were red, and the tops of her cheeks were speckled from the salty tears. She excused herself to the bathroom before the final bow to splash cold water on her face. A little bit of concealer went a long way. *If only I had a pair of big sunglasses. Why did I come here?*

As patrons streamed out of the front doors, Jenae stood by and looked for Logan to say goodbye. He walked up quickly to her side and said, "Are you alright?"

"The musical hit me really hard. Sorry I've been so emotional, it caught me by surprise," Jenae said.

"Where are you parked? Can I walk you to your car?" Logan asked.

"I'm in this garage, on the top floor." Jenae pointed to the cement structure across the street.

"My car is parked there too." Logan walked Jenae to the elevator and watched her get into her Camry under the yellow streetlights from afar. As soon as she drove off, he got back into the elevator to the ground floor, where he caught a cab home.

The next weekend, Jenae worked her usual twelve-hour day shifts on the cardiovascular unit at the big medical center by Golden Gate Park. She parked along the big boulevard that bordered the park because it was free, although the hike up the hill to the hospital got her heart racing and gave her a dewy sheen on her forehead. From her backpack, she pulled out two large, sweet oranges and a can of Diet Coke. She ate the oranges at a fast clip as she took report from the night shift. Her technique for cutting oranges made individual pyramid pieces that fit easily in her mouth. She pulled the fruit off the peel with her front teeth without spilling a drop of juice.

Her day was more eventful than usual. For the first time in her career, she almost passed out in a patient's room, while helping a surgeon change the dressing on a post cholecystectomy (gall bladder removal) patient. The patient was staying in a coveted solarium room that had amazing views of the bay, but got really warm with the sun streaming in the windows at the right angle. Jenae was gowned up and covered head to toe with a mask on as the doctor removed drainage tubes and cleaned out a large open wound. Sweat began to build up under her gown and she started to get dizzy and nauseated from the sun beating in on her back.

This is why I can't work in ICU. I really think I'm claustrophobic.

Jenae was relieved when the doctor asked for more clean gauze and bandages. She darted for the door, ripping off her gown and mask, and bent over as she leaned against the hallway wall. The cool air that entered her lungs kept her from losing consciousness and she asked a passing nurse to get more supplies and to finish assisting the doctor for her.

The day couldn't get any worse until she walked down the hill after her shift. It was dusk and as she approached her car from the sidewalk, she saw a note left on her windshield under the driver's side wiper.

Oh shit. Did I get a parking ticket? No, it's a note. But it's from the police.

The note said that her car had been involved in an accident and she was to call a number to get more details. From the passenger side where she walked up the sidewalk, the car looked fine. As she walked into the street and looked at the driver's side, the entire left side of her car had been smashed and the car was indeed un-drive-able.

Jenae moved back to the sidewalk and sat down on the curb as she reread the note. She slowly shook her head and stared down at her feet. She read the address of the nearest police station and looked up. It was directly across the street from where her car was parked. The wooden log cabin looking building looked more like a park ranger station than a satellite police station. She walked across the street and pounded on the locked door, but nobody answered. The walk home was tiring, but it took her mind off of her disappointing day and gave her time to plan her trip to New Zealand in her head to see Neve again.

Chapter 18

Big Gestures

The direct flight to Auckland, New Zealand, and then to Christchurch from San Francisco, seemed surprisingly cheap to Jenae, until she realized that the last week of June was the beginning of winter for the southern hemisphere. She was basically catching a ride on the produce and cargo flight. Her cheap ticket bought her the entire back third of the aircraft and she had her very own flight attendant. Both were happy with that arrangement. Jenae had gone to Trader Joe's to pick up cheap bottles of wine and snacks for Neve's family. The gifts were safely checked in her big suitcase stored underneath the plane. She figured they wouldn't know the difference between two-buck chuck and a fancy bottle of wine, since most of his family had never been to the States before.

Jenae moved to the front center seat in direct view of the movie screen for her own private showings. When she got peckish, the flight attendant brought her a meal or snacks, as well as complimentary alcoholic beverages. She was able to sleep a solid five hours before waking up to a sore hip and lower back. She felt like she was in a large, metal time machine hurling through space. Her destiny was completely out of her own control; she hoped that the pilots in front were awake and well trained. If it were up to her to land the plane, she would face certain death in a spectacular fireball.

Before landing, Jenae took a quick whore's bath with some disposable wipes from the flight attendant. She had heard mixed opinions on the cleanliness of the water stored on the plane for the bathroom and didn't want to take any chances. After reapplying her makeup, she spritzed on perfume, and tried to style her hair with a tiny comb. Neve wouldn't be in Auckland when she landed, but he suggested that she take the outside walkway from the international terminal to the domestic one, where she would catch her next flight to Christchurch.

Customs went much smoother than Jenae thought it would. Her massive suitcase full of wine and goodies didn't raise any red flags. Luckily, they just asked Jenae questions without opening up her baggage.

"Welcome to New Zealand," the large Maori official said.

"Thanks, it was a long flight," Jenae responded.

"Where are you coming from?"

"The U.S."

"Why are you here?"

"To visit my friend and his family."

"Do you have a return ticket?"

"Yes, I go back in four weeks."

"Where's your final destination?"

"Christchurch. I have the address."

"That was my next question."

"Do you have any live plants or animals in your possession?"

"No, sir."

"Enjoy your stay. The domestic terminal is that way."

"Thank you!" Jenae was excited to have a new passport stamp and relieved to have her feet on solid ground.

New Zealand had a different aroma as Jenae breathed in fresh air on her wake up walk to the gate where a little plane would take her to her to the South Island. The temperature was cool, and a light rain made her hair curl to a natural wave. Jenae's large rolling suitcase fell over in the crosswalk as she juggled her purse and two other bags. After struggling to right the roller bag, she put the bigger duffel bag on top of it, and lopped another gym bag over her shoulder that was filled with heavy shoes. *I should've packed better. I guess should just be glad that I made it.*

The layover for her next flight was quick, she had forty-five minutes left to wait once she reached the gate to Christchurch. A stop at the money exchange counter was easy, and rechecking her bags was no problem. The U.S. dollar was very close in value to the New Zealand dollar. Jenae wasn't sure if it was lunchtime or dinnertime, but she was hungry, and her tummy rumbled for something of substance. She looked around and found a shop selling savory pastries that were warmed by yellow-orange heating bulbs in a glass case. The shop offered three different kinds of food: sausage rolls, meat pies, and something with scrambled eggs peeking out the side. Jenae ordered one sausage roll and one meat pie with toasted sesame seeds on top to go. Grease from the sausage seeped through the brown bag, leaving dark splotches on the outside of it. She planned to eat it on the plane during the hour and a half flight on the final leg of her trip, and get a drink from the flight attendant. A distinguished, slim older gentleman with a thin mustache and a felt plaid hat excused himself to squeeze into the window seat next to Jenae. She hopped out of her seat to let him in as she bent her neck down in the aisle of the plane to avoid bumping her head on the ceiling.

"Hi, how are you?" Jenae greeted.

"Well, hello, young lady. Where is your accent from? Canada?"

"Oh, no. I just flew in from America. I started in San Francisco yesterday, I think."

"What an exciting trip. And you are going all the way to Christchurch?"

"Yes, my boyfriend is a New Zealander; he's from there. This is my first time here. I'm meeting his family and seeing where he grew up."

"How nice. Welcome! Do you know much about New Zealand?"

"Not really, just what I've heard from my boyfriend."

"I can tell you a little bit about the geography if you like. I'm a professor at the university in Christchurch, and I'm well versed in hydroelectricity. In fact, I'm coming back from a conference about hydrothermal energy."

The flight went by in a flash, between eating the tasty sausage roll and learning all about geography in New Zealand.

The professor gave her a snapshot dissertation:

The North Island was formed by volcanic activity, which is why smelly sulfur hot springs are prolific, especially in the Rotorua area. White Island, in the Bay of Plenty, just northwest of Auckland, shows signs of volcanic activity and could blow in the next century. Cook Strait, the gap between the North and South Islands, is known for its treacherous currents. A few ferries cross it every day between the Capitol, Wellington, and the small town of Picton. The cost for a ferry ride is less than a plane ticket, but the three-and-a-half-hour boat ride is best for tourists looking for a scenic route. Vacationers with camper vans find it handy.

The South Island was formed by a completely different phenomenon than the volcanic North Island; much like California. Both are on the border of the Pacific Plate and are susceptible to earthquakes because they plate-shift opposite of each other and create big mountains and deep ocean drop offs. The South Island has snowcapped mountains in the winter and big glaciers year-round. Whales are always hanging off the coast of Kaikoura. The Humpback and Southern Right whales migrate in during the winter months to fatten up on the big tuna and other rich seafood. Small penguins can be found at the south end of the island.

The plane banked over downtown Christchurch on final approach for landing. The professor pointed out his university and the many pointy stone structures that made Christchurch more English than England.

"Thanks for the tour and geography lesson. I'm going to wow Neve's family with all my newfound knowledge," Jenae said.

"It was a real pleasure to talk to you. Usually, I just sit in silence on these flights. Cheerio!"

The distraction on the final plane ride to see Neve was welcomed. Jenae was nervous; she was always so excited to see his smile and she couldn't wait to feel him in her arms again. The opportunity to meet his family opened the door for a more permanent future together, which created another set of anxieties for her. She pulled out her comb one more time and coifed her hair. She found the little box of Altoids in her purse and sucked on two very potent peppermint lozenges to hide the aroma of sausage roll.

Chapter 19

Kiwi Hospitality

Jenae walked off the plane onto the jetway, and into the arms of Neve waiting for her front and center in the gate area. His smile was wide, and chuckled as he bear-hugged her and lifted her off of her feet. He made a guttural, "Umgh." Neve felt so good that his body talked without him realizing it. Jenae squealed and held his face in her hands as she kissed his face all over.

"I made it! Boy that was a long flight. The earth is gigantic," Jenae said.

"The technology to fly that far is amazing! Let me look at your face. I still can't believe you made it all the way to little New Zealand," Neve said.

"Tell me, what do you have planned for us? Can I get a tour of the city?"

"First, I want to take you to a hotel where we can relax, and you can get some sleep. It has a hot tub in the room."

"Ah, that sounds nice. When do I get to meet your family?"

"We'll be staying at my mum's while you are here. I hope that's OK. I planned our first night at a hotel because Mum probably won't leave you alone to recuperate. She has a lot of questions."

"She sounds lovely."

"She has good intentions, but she's nosey. I love my mum; her name is Helen by the way, in case you forgot."

"Helen, OK. And your dad is Peter, right?"

"Yep, he goes by Pete. It may be next week before we see him. He's got a girlfriend, and I think he's on holiday with her at the moment."

"OK. Well, I'm ready to explore Christchurch."

Jenae approached the little Mitsubishi hatchback on the right front, and Neve chuckled and put his arms around her and led her to the other side and opened the door for her.

"We drive on the left side of the road, and the driver sits on the right side of the car," Neve said.

"Oh, I forgot. Mail trucks in the U.S. sit on the right side too, to deliver letters without having to get out of the truck."

Neve drove the stick shift down the main road, away from the airport and straight into town. Christchurch was charming with the stone churches and government buildings.

"That must be the university where my seat-mate from the plane works."

"I like that you are making friends!"

"What is your flying lesson schedule going to look like this month?"

"I've done a lot of bookwork and studying since I have been back. I'll start getting some practical flying experience soon, so you can come out to the airfield with me, at least to drop me off."

"How are you paying for this? I heard that flight instruction and airtime was really expensive."

"It is with fuel and instructor costs, and it is all out of pocket. I've taken out a loan, and I rented out my house. That's why we are staying at my mum's. Sorry about that."

"Are you doing construction on real estate flips, too? That seems like a lot."

"No, I put that on hold for now, and I'm learning how to trade stocks from a friend of mine. I hope the little bit of money I have will grow exponentially without breaking my back."

Neve drove past his mum's house where they'd be staying. He didn't have the intention of stopping-in to say "hello," but Jenae insisted. Helen was caught off guard; they found her in her garden turning over the soil to put it to bed for the winter. She was wearing a cloth hat with a string tightened around her neck to keep it in place.

Helen quickly stood up, dusted off the backside of her dark brown coveralls, and pulled off her gloves inside out. She walked up to Jenae and gave her a big hug. Jenae felt warmth in her heart and held both of Helen's hands and looked her in the eyes.

"I'm so excited to meet you and all your family. Neve has told me so much about you."

"Well, he's told us all about you, too. You're good as gold. Hamish will vouch for that too," Helen said.

"Thanks for letting me stay with Neve in your house. It's lovely by the way," Jenae said.

"It's not big, but it's new. Neve's dad built it for me, even though we've been divorced for so long. I think he got bored and needed a project. The price was right, anyway. He's built a lot of the houses in this neighborhood. I think you'll like it; it's close to the shopping area. I walk or bike over for the exercise."

"It seems like we aren't too far from downtown. Could I walk there if Neve is off doing his training?" Jenae asked.

"Yeah, sure. It'll take you about twenty minutes, but part of it is along the river, so it's a lovely stroll," Helen replied.

"OK chatty hens, we need to check into the hotel now. You'll have all month to figure that out together," Neve interrupted.

The hotel wasn't far from the boy's school that Neve attended. He pointed out the path he used to walk from his family home before his parents split up. The main thing he remembered about the house was that his father drank and yelled a lot. Neve's relationship with his dad was, at the very least, strained.

The lodging that Neve picked out was a modern-looking structure that had been built in the sixties. Neve chose it because it was the only hotel in town that offered a hot tub in the room. A neighborhood had grown up around it, which made it feel out of place. They checked in and Jenae immediately hit the shower to get the airplane germs off her body. Neve respectfully waited on the bed after he sprinkled rose petals along the carpet leading up to the bed and on the bedspread. He set a bottle of massage oil on the side table and lit a candle in a glass holder. As soon as he heard Jenae drying off from her shower, he opened a bottle of chilled champagne. She heard the "POP" as she walked out of the bathroom with a towel around her body and one twisted around her head; Neve approached her with a glass of champagne and gave her a gentle kiss on her lips.

"A toast to the most beautiful woman I know."

"Cheers to the sexiest and handsomest man that I will ever know," Jenae said as she raised and lowered her eyebrows.

Neve looked into Jenae's eyes and took a sip without breaking his gaze. After Jenae drank half of her glass, she got lightheaded, and Neve leaned in for another kiss. He took her glass and put it on the bedside table next to his and slipped his hands behind her neck and untwisted her hair wrap. He kissed her on her left neck, and then her right. He moved to her right clavicle and then to her left. Jenae felt her body surge with desire, and she ran her fingers through Neve's thick, dark hair. Her bosom engorged and released the damp towel from around her breasts and it fell to her feet. Neve kicked it away and confidently, grabbed both of her butt cheeks, one in each hand, and pulled her to him. He pressed his lips to hers, and she opened her mouth to feel the fullness of his passion.

Neve lifted her up and pulled her open legs up to his waist and his aching loins just before they fell sideways on the bed. Jenae pulled off his shirt first, then unbuttoned his jeans. She teased him by sitting on top of him and dropping her breasts toward his gapping mouth and pulling up before they touched his lips. He laughed and rolled her onto her back as he kicked his pants off. Neve lost the flow of the moment when he had to stop to remove his jeans caught on his ankles. He got his momentum back and showed Jenae the many ways he missed her. She was grateful for his generosity and fell asleep in Neve's arms; they spooned until the morning.

At dawns light they made love again and it was sweeter and more tender. Neve brought her a fresh coffee from the minibar with two creamers while she lay in bed. She mixed the cup with a small spoon and set it on the saucer. The sound of a metal spoon clinking on a porcelain plate was a foreign to her. She couldn't remember the last time she had a saucer under her cup. In America, she almost always used a paper or Styrofoam cup. *It's so much classier, or Old World here. I love it.*

A romp in the hot tub got them in the mood to take a run around Hagley Park, which was just down the block. They crossed a small babbling brook on a pedestrian bridge to reach the running path that circled the seven-mile perimeter. Jenae had left her Walkman behind in her suitcase because she wanted to communicate with Neve, even though she could barely breathe at the pace he was keeping. When they reached the courts, teenaged girls were playing a version of basketball, but they didn't dribble the ball, and the goal didn't have a backboard.

"Yeah, that's Netball, it's a girl's game."

"It looks harder than regular basketball," Jenae gasped.

"Coming up around the corner is a nice lake with some benches. We can take a break there if you want." Neve knew Jenae was at her limit. She wiped the sweat from her reddened face and walked over to the public water fountain to take some big gulps and splash water on her face and down her neck. Even though the weather was cool, she needed the break. Neve waited for her and stretched his calves as he leaned against the backside of the metal bench.

"Are you OK?" Neve asked.

"Oh yeah, I'm fine. Thanks for stopping for a drink. I think I'm a little bit dehydrated from the flight."

A canoe with a middle-aged couple rowed past. They seemed stoic until the lady touched the surface of the water and lightly splashed the man behind doing all the paddling. He faked a whimper and sprinkled cool lake water on her back in return. She giggled.

"We can take a short cut back and I'll show you where the botanical gardens are. It would be a good place for you to explore while I'm training this month," Neve said.

"I may have to work on my running here. It's ideal with flat unending paths and beautiful views."

They ran all the way to the end of the park from where they started and cooled down on the walk back to the hotel. Checkout wasn't until 2 PM, just enough time to hop in the hot tub one more time.

⋅◦⋅

On the drive to Helen's house, they stopped by Hamish's duplex. Neve had been staying with Hamish since his return to New Zealand, but the brothers agreed that it wasn't big enough to house three adults comfortably. Jenae was worried that Hamish didn't appreciate Neve's girlfriend always being around until he explained their younger sister was going to move in temporarily until she could live with her soon to be fiancé.

"You'll get to meet Tee, our youngest sister, next time you come by. She has new golden retriever puppy and needs to live in a place with a garden," Hamish said.

"Mum wants to host a dinner at her house later this week and wants all of her kids there; I think my aunts are invited too," Neve said.

"Excellent, I can't wait," Jenae said as she felt the pressure to become a perfect daughter-in-law. She still didn't know if the whole thing would work out.

Neve and Jenae returned from the grocery store to pickup last-minute ingredients for their special dish from the U.S., a mounded plate of nachos. Jenae had found tortilla chips, a pound of ground beef, grated cheddar cheese, sour cream, tomatoes, and peppers, along with an avocado.

Neve walked into the front room of Helen's home holding Jenae's hand behind him. He grinned and greeted his aunts, an uncle, and some cousins who had already downed a few gin and tonics. They seemed more excited to meet an American than anything. After they set the bags of groceries in the kitchen, Helen introduced Jenae to everyone. Jenae reached her hand out, but they pulled her in and kissed her cheek instead of a handshake. Shaking hands was not a custom there, and it was a sign that an American was on the other side of it. Neve found the gesture endearing. After unexpected compliments from the extended family died down, Neve explained what "right as rain" and "good as gold" meant. They escaped to the kitchen to make an American sized platter of nachos for the guests.

"My friend Sara and I made this recipe up in high school after sports practice. She played basketball, and I swam. I was always starving after swim practice."

"Nachos in New Zealand are pronounced with the 'na' like in 'batch' not 'nah' in 'botch.' And we would only put single chips down with a few pieces of grated cheese on each one with maybe a tomato cube," Neve said.

"OK, watch and learn. We fry up the ground beef in the skillet and add chopped onion and garlic. Then we dump the entire bag of chips onto a roasting pan or cookie sheet. Drain the meat, and strategically place it on the mound of chips. Nothing is single file in American nachos."

"It looks like we could feed the neighborhood with this monstrosity!"

"Yes, or . . . a couple of hungry high school girls. Next, we top with grated cheddar cheese and put it under the broiler on low for a few minutes. Keep an eye on it so the chips don't burn but the cheese needs to get melted and gooey."

"Should I make the salsa while it cooks?"

"Sure, I'll make the guacamole. Where's the lemon? Ah, I see it."

The American nachos were glorious with the colors of the Mexican flag; green guacamole, white sour cream and red salsa topped the mound of chips, meat, beans, and cheese.

The party broke up before 10 PM and shortly after, slightly inebriated, Helen, retired to her bedroom after giving a quick wave to her children on her way up the stairs. "Goodnight loves!"

The siblings hung out in the living room and told stories about one another, the funniest ones for Jenae to hear were about Neve's childhood. He was a mama's boy and was doted on by his oldest sister who dressed him in fancy flannel shorts, with suspenders, and knee-high wool socks with leather shoes. A photo album pulled from a shelf confirmed the stories. He was a talented boxer in his primary years and became a better runner and compulsory cricket player like every young boy in the country.

Seemingly happy family memories of birthdays, Christmas, and vacations were captured in pictures stuck in that book, but each offspring eventually shared a negative opinion about Peter, their angry drunken father. On Friday nights after handing out pay envelopes to his workers, he headed to the local pub to meet his friends to drink away half of his profits. Helen stayed home and made do for the family by stretching meals out for the week, especially when Peter went on an extensive binger. Neve assured Jenae that she would have the pleasure of meeting him sometime soon.

Jenae's initial impression of New Zealand took her back to the 1960s. They didn't have the usual, standard amenities of American homes in the late eighties. Despite the promise of hydroelectric power, electricity, and water were diligently conserved. Low utility use was more evident in the cold of the winter. Central heat was not common in most New Zealand homes, and Helen had two small portable radiators on casters that she moved around with her to keep her feet warm. A blanket over her shoulder and lap helped maintain body heat, too. Jenae was surprised and impressed to see that Helen hung her laundry out to dry on the lines in the backyard even though the temperatures were close to zero degrees Celsius. Short hot showers were encouraged with three adults under one roof, which was a problem for Neve. Jenae was quick to get rinsed off first thing in the morning because Neve enjoyed lingering in the warm spray until it turned lukewarm. Any water after Neve's shower ran cold until the water heater could work its magic a few hours later. Despite her cold toes, Jenae felt comfortable with the warmth of Neve's family.

Chapter 20

Agriculture and Alps

Neve's soon to be brother-in-law was a resident farmer on a ranch just outside of Christchurch. He came from an affluent family in town. Bill and Tee were planning on marriage, but were waiting for more financial stability. Jenae was excited to visit a sheep farm and shoot guns, at least that was the plan when Neve and Jenae drove out to the country on an early, misty morning. Tee and Bill met them outside a small cabin and waved them to park next to the dog kennels. Tee wore sweatpants and an oversized flannel shirt over long underwear. Bill wore big, rubber gum boots already muddied from morning chores. He looked like a proper farmer, even though he grew up in the poshest house in Christchurch with six siblings.

"Yeah, right. Are you two city dwellers ready to get dirty? I see you've worn the wrong shoes, Jenae. You're not going to get very far in those patent leather buckled numbers, are ya?" Bill teased.

"I'll get you a pair of my boots, I think we're about the same foot size," Tee offered.

"Thanks Tee. I didn't think to pack boots; I guess I should've asked," Jenae said.

"No worries, Jenae. I had to borrow a pair of trekkers from Hamish," Neve said.

The foursome put on jackets before Bill gave them a tour of the dog kennels.

"Over here, we have six herding dogs. The two young border collies are siblings, and this is their mum, Rizzo." Bill pointed to the dogs relaxing in beds of hay under a rudimentary shelter.

Jenae walked toward the dogs to get a better look and started to tell them how handsome and smart they were.

"Hey, hey. Those dogs aren't pets. They're working dogs. We don't baby-talk them, or pet them, or let them in the house. They are here to work and they love it. We don't want to confuse them," Bill said.

"Oh, sorry. They are just so cute; muddy, but sweet," Jenae said.

"No worries. We only have one pet on this farm, and she only comes on the weekends with Tee. She's the most spoilt animal, I've ever known. She can't be with the working dogs, or they might get soft like her," Bill said. Tee's golden retriever walked close to the group and got lots of pats on the head from Jenae and Tee.

Bill loaded everyone up into a covered four-wheel utility vehicle and surveyed the entire property for lost sheep and checked the perimeter fence line for breaches and breakages. Two of the herding dogs followed alongside the four-wheeler at a consistent speed of 50 KPH. They smiled the whole way while running full speed, until Bill stopped at a galvanized stock tank. The dogs leapt into the tanks to cool off and lapped up drinks of water from the surface.

"This is their favorite part of the job. This and herding sheep. Let's go find the herd," Bill said.

"Tee, can you drive the cart back to the house while I guide the dogs to move these sheep to the next field?" Bill asked.

"Sure. Now this is my favorite part of being out here. Driving through the fields," Tee said.

Bill sauntered into the field of high grasses toward the flock of sheep. He put his pointer and pinky fingers in his mouth and made whistling noises to instruct the dogs on position and speed when approaching the sheep. Bill shouted semi-comprehensible words to his two border collies, Jasper and Millie, while the others watched from the ATV.

"Hup, hup. Woah, lay. Give 'em room to find the exit."

Sheep huddled next to the fence line of the muddied grass field. Bill opened a fence up to allow the sheep to enter a narrow path that led to a new pasture of planted turnips. Dogs followed the sheep, then Bill, and then Tee driving the ATV. A careful balance of crops needed to be planted to free range feed his livestock. Grass, the main feed of sheep, didn't grow in the winter, and Bill had figured out how to supplement with turnips and maize to make sure the sheep were healthy, especially for the soon to be expectant ewes.

Once the ewes delivered their lambs about 145 days after servicing; they were kept in a special shelter with extra straw and feed to keep milk production up for lambs to grow strong. The rest of the flock were placed in a protected shelter at night during inclement weather. Sheep dogs were the key to moving livestock from one field to another or separating the sick from the weak.

The foursome returned to the small cottage and warmed their feet next to the stove pipe stove in the corner of the kitchen. Bill threw a few sticks of wood into its belly, and the flames put out substantial heat. Tee poured a spot of tea out of the electric kettle and served it in China cups and saucers. She grabbed a sleeve of digestive biscuits, which Jenae compared the taste to animal crackers back home. They were delicious and addictive when submerged into hot tea.

"How do you like the farm life, Tee? Answer carefully, because Bill seems to like it and it is his profession of choice," Neve asked.

"I visit Bill on the weekends and maybe once during the week I'll bring him dinner, so it's good, yeah. I feel good that the sheep are used for their wool. I couldn't look at the sweet beings knowing that we were sending them out for slaughter when they got enough meat on their bones," Tee said.

"I imagine it's magical here in the summertime; with the green fields against the mountain range in the background. It's beautiful now, in the winter," Jenae said.

"Yeah, yeah, yeah. It's easier to work outside in the summertime, too. Right, I need to give the dogs their deworming medicine for the month. Do you want to help me with that Jenae, since you are the nurse I'm sure you're used to that," Bill said.

"I'd love to. I bet the patients are easier than my usual ones," Jenae said.

Tee and Neve stayed in the cottage to chat more and discuss possible future in-laws. Jenae and Bill donned their boots again and trudged to the working dog kennels. On a tree stump, Bill cut large discs off a meat roll with a big butcher knife. He usually fed each dog five or six discs each meal, but this time he smashed a deworming pill in the middle of one. He opened a couple of metal cages, threw the meat discs in, and watched the first two dogs chomped them down in delight. He handed Jenae the rest and opened each individual cage while she tossed the meat disc into the air for each dog to catch.

"Tee told me that you worked in labor and delivery. Have you ever been to a lambing in the springtime?" Bill asked.

"No, it sounds fun though."

"Yeah, these ladies usually give birth to two or three at a time and sometimes they need help releasing the lamb from the birth canal. It's a busy time making sure the lambs are nursing and the mums get enough nourishment."

"It sounds intense."

"If you come back to visit, I'll loan you some gum boots and coveralls and you can help me get the job done," Bill said.

"It's funny, I've never thought I'd ever visit New Zealand, but now that I've been here, I can see that it's a nice laid-back place to live," Jenae said.

<hr />

"I promised we'd go shooting. Now that the sheep are on the other side of the ranch, we can shoot from right over that fence. I have some cans already set up on the next fence line," Bill said to the group as he led them to the property line. He carried two long shot guns cocked open with shells and had ear plugs in the pockets of his canvas coat.

"Neve, you should be good at this. Didn't you train at the police academy with rifles and stuff?" Tee asked.

Jenae knew that this was a sensitive subject since Neve shot and killed a man in the line of duty and still carried the psychological scars. He had only shared that part of his life with Hamish, Jenae, and the department's psychiatrist. She felt horrible that Neve still suffered in silence.

"I'll go first. I've never shot a gun before, but I heard that it's loud and the butt of the gun can hurt," Jenae said.

"Put your ear plugs in, and let me show you how to hold the gun against the meaty part of your shoulder, so it won't hurt so much," Neve said.

Jenae held her left eye to the sight line, and placed her right finger on trigger, and rested the long barrel of the gun on top of the fence rail. She could barely see the half dozen cans sitting 25 meters away. She shot once and although a bullet left the gun, nothing happened. The tin cans didn't move, and she didn't hear a sound—no ricochet or anything. She shot again and got the same result.

"I'm not hitting anything, and it's painful," Jenae said. Tee took a few shots and hit one can. Neve declined the opportunity without explaining why he hadn't picked up a firearm since his work shooting. Bill shot all five cans left sitting on the fence, missing only once.

As the sun came out, Jenae pulled two bottles of chardonnay out of the boot of the car that Neve and she had gotten on a wine tour earlier in the week. Tee ran in the cottage and grabbed some mason jars and a corkscrew to open the wine. As they sat at the wooden picnic table under a big silver beech tree, they toasted and laughed louder and louder as the booze took effect.

⚬

While Neve studied aviation and took instructional flights at the airfield, Jenae developed a routine in the mornings. She had a cup of Earl Gray tea and a scone freshly made by Helen every morning. Jenae's favorite was blueberry, but was fine with raisin, since fresh fruit was hard to come by in the winter months. She had two cassettes that she listened to in her portable tape player while she ran with black foam earpieces on her head set. The bulk of every morning was spent in Hagley Park. Running in the cool mist made her feel like she could go forever, and she typically ran the entire seven miles, which meant listening to some Phil Collin's songs twice. His beat was a good pacer for warm up, sprints, and cool downs. She took advantage of having no responsibilities; no work, no papers due, and no tests; just time to work on Jenae and her relationship with Neve. She met Tee for lunch downtown and shopped for souvenirs. Her favorite purchase was an All Blacks jersey from the local sports fan store. She had learned the NZ TV schedule fairly easily. Three-day cricket matches were broadcast over the weekends. Wheel of Fortune New Zealand was on every weeknight at dinnertime with a tall blonde letter turner like Vanna. She was younger and liked to talk about her fighter pilot husband. It was very similar to the U.S. version, but the prizes were smaller, and the contestants looked scared and shy, unlike boisterous camera-ready Americans.

— ◆ —

Neve finished another week of training and was getting close to getting the 20 hours flying instructor requirement before making his first solo flight. He was nervous about meeting that benchmark but enjoyed everything else about flying. On the 90-minute drive to Mount Hutt for a ski day, Jenae took in the view as Neve drove and gave a verbal diarrhea monologue of everything he had done in training that week. She tried to take it all in, assuming it helped him to retain the knowledge by repeating it out loud.

"This week my instructor took me out past the Waimakariri River, north of here, to practice steep turns and approach to stalls. We waved the wings back and forth to sixty degrees each way. Any further, like at ninety degrees, it's considered unusual attitude, and the plane can end up in a spin. He had me practice pitching the airplane down to pick up speed, and I'm getting good at controlling pitch and power."

"So, you pick up speed as you fall with gravity? That makes sense."

"Yeah, yeah, yeah. And that's really important for a smooth landing. So, when you are coming into land, you approach and pass the runway so you see it over your shoulder and wing at forty-five-degree angle, then turn back at a ninety degree angles. Then when you're lined up with the runway you descend at a three to one rate and should see one-third ground and two-third sky. Before you touchdown you flare the nose up about five feet to where you see sky and ground fifty-fifty."

"How fast are you going?" Jenae asked.

"We land at seventy knots, and the cool thing is you aim to land on markings on the runway called captain bars, but there are also PAPI lights on the runway that indicate if you are good or not. Two reds and two whites are good. Four red lights mean you are too low, and four white lights means you are too high. I freaked out and my knees went weak when I made an approach and had to pull up and go around because I was too high. I would have gone off the runway into the fence," Neve explained.

"I'm so proud of you, it sounds like you are really good at flying. It is really flowing for you, which means you are on the right path."

"I'm glad I gave up flipping houses for investing in the stock market, too. I've been able to keep afloat by trading a few stocks on the FTSE exchange."

"Isn't that the UK exchange?" Jenae asked.

"Yeah, yeah. You forget that New Zealand is a small country. We still rely on the mother country," Neve said.

<hr>

The drive up to Mount Hutt was sporty, especially looking down shear face cliffs with no road barrier between the car sliding on the icy road and certain death. The ski rental center had cleared the morning crowd by the time Jenae and Neve showed up. The couple was happy to get a few hours on the slopes in. Neither were ski enthusiasts but enjoyed the outdoors and nature's beauty more. Jenae mostly loved spending time with Neve and learning new things about his personality. She had to stop herself from gazing too long and lovingly into his blue eyes as he told her stories. She was still mesmerized by his Kiwi British accent. Everything between her knees and neck got warm and tingly when she was with him.

The line to the lower chair lift was short, and Jenae just hoped she wouldn't fall as the chair came around and get knocked unconscious before she could get up the mountain. Neve helped her scoot to the back of the chair before pulling the safety bar over their laps. Her legs felt heavy as they swayed back and forth over skiers slaloming below. She forgot how much boots and skis weighed, it reminded her of moving dead bodies to the morgue and the extreme heaviness of literal dead weight.

They exited the chair halfway up the mountain without incident.

"Do you want to take the tow bar lift up to the top of that peak? We'll have a longer ski down if we do," Neve asked.

"I've never done a tow bar before. Is it hard to hang on?" Jenae said.

"Oh no, it's easy. You just stand with your legs bent and hang on to the bar. It drags you up the mountain on your skis," Neve said.

Neve and Jenae went straight to the front of the line, and Jenae wished she could watch more people maneuver the pole so she could learn from their technique.

"I'll go first so you can watch." Neve grabbed the pole and placed the crossbar through his legs and looked back.

Jenae followed him onto the next bar and was successful while she kept her legs and butt engaged as the motor at the top of the hill pulled them up the slope. As Neve looked back, a young boy in front of him fell in the tow bar path, and Neve tumbled over the top of him and off trail. Jenae screamed as her skis bumped into the red-faced lad. The lift operator stopped additional skiers from entering the line until the coast was clear. Neve and Jenae let out wails of laughter with their skis vertical as they laid on the snowy mountain.

Chapter 21

Last Night and Flight

Neve booked the same hotel room with a hot tub for Jenae's last night on her visit to Christchurch. She had to get back for a summer-session classes and put in some hours at the hospital to get her bank account back up and running. It was gasping on fumes with the cost of living in San Francisco and tuition. Helen helped her with her bags and said goodbye with a hug and a smile. She was especially happy to get most of her house back because she had a secret boyfriend who had been feeling left out.

At the hotel room, Neve asked Jenae to dress up for an early, fancy dinner. He'd made reservations at a five-star restaurant located in a historical hotel in the middle of town. They were the only couple seated in the high-ceilinged ballroom. It felt like a cathedral to Jenae. The servers were attentive and quickly brought wine and hors d'oeuvres. Neve pointed out figures on the painted ceiling high above them. Jenae felt like she was in a dream. She imagined getting engaged in a setting like this, with the ring hidden in glass of champagne or a serving of Pavlova.

She knew she loved Neve, but she wasn't ready for marriage, not yet. Just like with all her other boyfriends . . . not yet.

When dessert was placed on the table by the head server with white gloves, Neve asked for Jenae's hands and held them gently across the round table.

He looked into her eyes and said, "I'm so happy that you came here to meet my family and stay with me to see where I come from. My mom loves you, and Tee may be a little jealous of you, but I think you made a good impression on them."

"I really like your family as well. They were sweet and welcoming, even your dad. I was expecting a big ogre," Jenae said.

"Dad's gotten more subdued in his old age. I'm starting to like him, too."

"The Neve I see here makes sense to me now. You have a strong foundation, but you also have big dreams. It's important that I'm with someone who has a big life, because that's what I want for myself," Jenae said.

"That makes me happy to hear you say that, because more than anything I want you to know that I love you, Jenae; with all my heart."

Jenae's face beamed and her cheeks glowed as she parted her lips and gripped his hands tighter.

She leaned in and stared into Neve's eyes. "I love you too, Neve. You make me so happy."

Neve pushed his chair from the table, stood up and walked to Jenae. She turned and lifted her arms up to his neck, and Neve leaned down to give her a passionate kiss. Servers magically turned around and retreated to the kitchen. Jenae felt like a princess, for the first time a man she loved treated her like one.

❖

The evening of love making back at the hotel room started in the hot tub and continued through half the night. It was as if they wanted to bank passion for the future months, they would be away from each other.

Jenae had a full two semesters of business school ahead of her and Neve was looking at fifteen more months of pilot training and flying hours before he would be eligible to be hired by a regional jet.

"At least we can both concentrate on our educations without being distracted by each other. Maybe you can come back to the U.S. to visit at Christmas time and meet my family," Jenae said.

"That'd be great. I guess I'll have to see what's gone wrong with my visa to get back into the U.S."

"I think I have someone who can look into it. I'll check with them when I get back," Jenae said.

"Thanks. Until I can come visit you, I'll be working on my solo flights and instrument training. It's really important for moving forward in this career," Neve said.

Jenae was a little annoyed that Neve was prioritizing flying over her, but realized that she was doing the same thing to him. She wasn't engaged yet and didn't anticipate a ring popping up before she was finished with graduate school.

Goodbye at the airport was treated like a see-you-later as they gave each other teary-eyed hugs. Neither wanted to let go, and Neve's stomach hurt as he watched Jenae enter the jetway to the plane.

⚊⚊◆⚊⚊

The flight back to SFO seemed longer than Jenae's trip to New Zealand. Her mindset was that she had nothing good to look forward to—except spending time with her friends. But in reality, she didn't mind working or studying hard; it made her feel useful and important.

She formulated a plan to contact Logan when she landed to see if he had any luck in determining the status of Neve's visa, and had no plans to give her secret away to Neve. She knew he would be livid. *What he doesn't know won't hurt him*, she thought.

The ride back to her apartment on a blue and yellow shuttle van was efficient and totally worth the $8. Jenae almost forgot that her busted up car was still at the body shop. She wondered if the insurance company would agree to repair her reliable little Camry or deem it "totaled." Either way, it was a pain in the ass.

Paulina was out when Jenae returned to the apartment, but there were several Post-It notes stuck on her door: one with the phone number of the insurance guy, and two handwritten from Logan.

Jenae ignored the mail and bills piled up on her bed and put on her workout clothes and headed to campus. She picked up her books from the campus bookstore and the syllabi for the classes she was taking in summer session. At the gym she found an empty stationary bike with a book holder on the handlebars and started reading her assignments, although friends from class were extra chatty as they leaned on her equipment and told her about summer classes. It felt good to get back, but she felt like she had entered the rat race of the big city in a huge country.

It was good and bad. Many of her friends had met Neve and were surprised that she was willing to keep the long-distance relationship going, especially the young single men in her classes. Once they learned that Neve was out of the country; tall, dark, Turkish, and sort of handsome, Zeki took charge and made it his mission to break their relationship up. Zeki asked Jenae to lunch at a local Chinese restaurant under the guise of discussing a group project in their summer class together.

"It's a good idea to eat and plan at the same time, right?" Zeki asked.

"Sure, I thought we'd meet on campus, but this is good. A chance to eat a hot meal."

Jenae ordered beef broccoli with white rice and potstickers. Zeki wasn't used to eating Chinese food and ordered a vegetable dish that resembled something he could get in Turkey. Zeki looked into the teapot, replaced the lid, and poured the weak hot liquid into little ceramic cups with no handles. As he offered a cup to Jenae, he barraged her with questions about why she was with a man who didn't even live in the same country.

What if she picked the wrong man by marrying too early in life? Jenae instantly regretted agreeing to lunch, and she was amazed at the gall and ego of the interrogation. Zeki had made his point. It felt like disrespect and stuck with her for a long time, but she figured that this man who barely knew her only brought it up because he wanted a chance to be with her.

His culture was different and although Jenae wasn't terribly religious, she knew she wanted to be yoked with a man who was raised in a Christian family; and Zeki didn't fit the bill.

⚬

Jenae's determination to get Neve back in the country was reinvigorated after Zeki's confrontation. She was offended that a man thought he knew what was best for her, mostly because she was a woman, and he was a man.

A call to Logan to check on the visa investigation for Neve turned into another innocent lunch—this time at a nicer restaurant with white table clothes in a tony part of town. Logan picked Jenae up at her apartment because she was car-less, and he offered to drop her off on campus in time for her classes. The waiter in all black brought them a carafe of cold-water beading down with condensation and a breadbasket with an assortment of olive oil and spice mixes. Logan placed a white-starched linen napkin on his lap and offered fresh focaccia to Jenae.

"So, tell me about your trip to New Zealand. How's Neville managing without you?"

"He's doing well and focused on aviation. He wants to work as a commercial pilot one day."

"I bet he really wants to get back into the U.S., huh?"

"I want him to be able to come back over. Did you find out anything on why his visa has been delayed?"

"Neville's application had some inconsistencies, and I'm having my good buddy in immigration give it another look. I know this is important to you, and I want to make you happy."

"Thanks Logan, I appreciate it."

"So, how's nursing going at the med center? You have a busy schedule between being a full-time student and working every weekend."

"The vacation helped a lot. I'm rested up and ready for the grind again. I've got bills to pay, so that keeps me going, too. I had a patient the other night who came in off of the street. The guys that abuse drugs use the hospital as a revolving door. The frequent fliers get brought in on an ambulance gurney, ER pumps their chests, and ICU stabilizes them. When they get to me, we detox them, they soak the grime off in a hot soapy bath, get rehydrated with a banana bag filled with B vitamins, fill their bellies with a few good meals, and then they're back out in the park until next time," Jenae said.

"That seems costly for the state," Logan said.

"I'm sure it isn't cheap—until the poor bastard doesn't make it out of the hospital. Back in Dallas, I had a similar patient in with back pain, which the orthopedic doctor was convinced that he was just trying to score narcotics. Anyway, the patient was an all-around bad dude and called me to his room to help him go to the bathroom, and then to sit in a chair. He seemed fine. Then, he called again just a few minutes later and wanted back into bed. When he was settled back in, he started freaking out and was talking to someone above the doorframe in the room. I looked around the corner into the hallway and didn't see anyone. He thrashed around and shouted out loud, 'No, Jesus, don't send me there! I can't go there. Please, Jesus!' His eyes got as big as saucers; then he died," Jenae explained.

"Wow!" Logan responded.

"Yeah, and I called a code and started chest compressions. The resident on call was flustered and basically moved him to ICU with a nurse riding the bed and giving CPR up the elevator. It was too late. The guy's soul had already moved on to his next eternal station. I'm assuming hell."

"Wow again!"

"I feel like I've witnessed heaven and hell. I've been with several people who have passed on, and all the others died peacefully, some with a smile on their faces. Not this guy," Jenae said.

"I've only seen dead bodies that have been murdered basically, and one suicide. I'm immune to the impact of a dead body. I have no emotions about it," Logan said.

"When someone passes in my presence, I consider it a privilege to be so close to the other side. I imagine that the veil is open at that moment. I always say a prayer for their soul to make it to heaven. In fact, when priests visit patients, I sneak into the room and pray with them. I'm not even Catholic. I figure some Graces might rub off on me," Jenae pontificated.

"You're made out of a different cloth than me then. I don't believe in heaven or hell or God or Jesus. They are made up characters to keep masses of people in line," Logan said.

"Well, one day we'll all find out, won't we? I not only believe in God, I know there's a God," Jenae said.

"I have reasons why I don't believe. I'll tell you about my messed-up childhood another time. Let's get out of here," Logan said.

Chapter 22

What Ifs

Zeki's words at lunch impacted Jenae more than she thought they would. She was sure that she loved Neve, but often wondered if they could they make it work in the long term.

Would love be enough to conquer all their challenges to be together? I'm already keeping secrets from him. He would hate that I have had any contact with Logan, but I'm doing it for him. Maybe he thinks it's too much, too. He has dreams for a big life, and he is going to need some room to achieve that. What if the immigration problems can't be fixed?

Temptations to date other men were all around Jenae at the hospital and in the MBA program. Two different doctors from different services had asked her out in the same week. One was big and boisterous and made her laugh, the other was steamy and sultry and commanded the room. Jenae humored Dr. Big by going on a "friend" bike ride with him in the Presidio. He used the excuse of stopping to look at the views one too many times. The hills had conquered his fitness level, and there was nothing sexy about a man having to stop in the middle of an incline to wipe his brow and catch his breath.

Dr. Sultry found her number at the hospital and called her at home. He wanted to talk, and to take her out. She was flattered and would have accepted if she hadn't been so loyal to Neve. She knew she wouldn't be able to resist his advances.

"We can go do something, like work out or play tennis . . . as friends," Jenae said.

"What do you mean as friends?" Dr. Sultry asked.

"I'm kind of dating someone seriously, and he's out of the country, so I have free time but just for a friendship."

"I'm not looking for a friend, Jenae."

His words excited Jenae and saddened her at the same time. *If only I was single, I could be hanging out with Dr. Sultry. Dammit.*

⸎

Sandy popped over to Jenae's apartment to hand over the keys to her BMW while she went out of town on a work trip. She felt sorry that Jenae's car got totaled, and she'd be on the East Coast for three weeks between training and visiting friends over the weekends. Jenae was grateful, but a little nervous to drive a luxury car since she had only owned a VW Bug and a Camry.

"I like your apartment. It's so cozy and close to the university," Sandy said.

"I can't believe you haven't been here before. You missed out on helping me move in I guess."

"Yeah, sorry about that. I'm not strong enough to move furniture. Who helped you?"

"The FBI guy who I met in Hawaii last summer. I keep running into him, and now we've become friends. He's helping me get Neve's visa sorted out so he can come back to the States."

"Oh yeah, you mentioned him before, in Santa Cruz. That's odd. You know men don't ever want to be just friends with women. How does Neve feel about your 'friendship?'"

"I haven't told him. I think he'd flip out."

"You're damn right, he'd flip out."

"Anyway, you should come to the REC Center with me as my guest sometime and build up your strength. The gym is one of the best in the city." Jenae tried to redirect the conversation.

"Yeah, I'm not big on weight training or classes. I like skiing and biking; maybe you can come to Tahoe with me sometime. Tell me about New Zealand. I've always wanted to go there. Was it rugged like in the movies?" Sandy said.

"It was nice even though it's winter there now. Neve's family treated me really well, and he finally told me that he loved me," Jenae said.

"Aw! I love that he loves you. Did you say it back?"

"Of course I did. I've loved him for a long time, but I wanted him to say it first."

"So, no drama or anything? You know you want to be with a guy that is steady Eddie, right? No drama?"

"The only drama was having to say goodbye. He's really into his aviation training and serious about becoming a commercial pilot. He won't be coming back here for at least a year," Jenae said.

"Like I've told you before, you need to take chances with confidence, and if he is the guy who makes you laugh when you want to cry, then he may be worth it. But never stay if he makes you cry. OK? Life is short and you're young and vibrant and I know you could have the pick of the litter of straight guys around here. Never settle," Sandy said.

"I'll keep that in mind. Communication is our biggest hurdle. We write letters, but the information is stale by the time they get read, and phone calls are outrageously expensive. It'd be cheaper to buy a flight every other month to visit. His birthday is coming up next week, and I'll call him for that, but he won't get an actual gift. It's too expensive to airmail, and by boat it can take month to get there."

"Honestly, you might be better off sticking with Neve if he's a good guy. The dates I've had lately have been atrocious."

"Oh yeah, tell me. I love hearing your stories."

"Well one guy asked me out, and I said yes. Then, I canceled on him last minute because I heard something about him through the grapevine. I made up some lame excuse. One of my best girlfriends took me to a house moving out party on Lombard Street on that same night. It was a big party, and I didn't know the owner, but it was wild, and we were spray painting the walls and crashing small appliances into the back garden from the balcony. Lo and behold, I turned around in the jam-packed kitchen and literally ran into this guy—chest to chest. Well, my face was to his chest because he was a big guy. But anyway, he was the one I canceled on for that very night. I was so embarrassed. We looked at each other, didn't say a word, and I got the hell out of there," Sandy said.

"Sometimes words are overrated," Jenae replied.

"And then last night, I went to dinner with this really nice engineer. I knew I probably wouldn't be attracted to him, but I wanted to try out a new restaurant and my motto is to try to learn something from my date that I didn't already know: Like how to fly fish or what it's like to catch a pass as an NFL player. So anyway, the guy is really nerdy and extra nice, but he knew he was out of his league. He walked me to my door and by the time we made it up the sidewalk, he was drenched in sweat. I mean, a stream of sweat was rolling down both cheeks and dripping off his jawline. No way was I giving him a goodnight kiss, not even on the cheek, ew!"

After Sandy's talk, Jenae was even more grateful for Neve.

⸻ ◆ ⸻

"Happy birthday to you, happy birthday to you. Happy birthday, dear Neve. Happy birthday to you . . . I LOVE

YOU!" Jenae sang the whole song without interruption when Neve answered the phone.

"Hello! Thanks Jenae. I love hearing your voice, and you sing like a lark too," Neve said.

"How's your day going? Are you taking some time to celebrate?"

"Yeah, a couple of my mates from the aviation classes took me out to the pub for a few pints. We were celebrating my birthday, but also taking a break from studying."

"Sounds like fun."

"Tonight, we are having a family gathering with cake and everything. I feel too old for that sort of thing, but Mum insisted."

"I wish I could be there. Give everyone my best, OK?"

"I will. How've you been? Missing me at all?"

"Of course I'm missing you. I got As in my summer session classes and we've already had one paper due in each class for this semester; time is passing so quickly because I'm so busy."

"Has anything come in the mail from immigration?" Neve asked.

"Not yet, but Logan is checking on your visa. He promised." Jenae coughed and choked on the words she spoke.

"Logan? The FBI guy, Logan?" Neve asked.

"Uh, yeah. Don't get mad, Neve. He said he could help," Jenae said sheepishly.

"How often do you talk to this guy? You know he hates me, right?"

"He acts like he wants to help us, though," Jenae said.

"Jenae! Stop being so naïve. This guy is a psychopath, and he is obsessed with you! I wouldn't be surprised if he's the reason why my visa is put on hold right now."

"Really? You think so? But he's been so nice to me. He helped me move into my apartment and took me to lunch to discuss your case. I think you are wrong about him. He's a really caring guy!"

"I'm so angry right now. Thanks for the birthday wishes. It really sounds like you have a thing for this Logan guy," Neve said.

"No, no, no, it's not that. I love you. I'm trying to help you!" Jenae said.

"I can't do this anymore," Neve said.

"What do you mean you can't do this anymore?"

"Maybe we need to take a break. I'm so pissed off, and I've got too much on my plate right now with pilot instruction. I'm starting my instrument training, and I have to master this to move forward to get my commercial rating. I need to remove all distractions so that I can concentrate," Neve said.

He could hear Jenae crying quietly, but she didn't say any words in response. She couldn't speak. Her heart was breaking.

"Jenae? Are you there?"

"I'm still here, but I'm really sad." Jenae knew that fixing this relationship would take a lot of hard work or an act of God.

She was numb all over and felt pressure building in her chest because she forgot to breathe.

"I guess we are taking a break then, Neve. Whatever that means," Jenae said.

"Yeah. Just consider yourself single. I can't wrap my head around you talking to Logan behind my back."

The words Neve spoke burned a hole into her heart. Jenae shook her head slowly and then faster and wider as the news sunk in. She thought, 'this just can't be, I can't believe this is happening.'

"OK, well enjoy your birthday. Bye." Jenae waited for him to change his mind.

"Bye." Neve had tears in his eyes when he loosened his grip on the phone receiver after he hung up it up. He felt tingling in his chest and stomach as he took a moment to process what had just happened with the woman he loved.

◆○◆

Jenae's voice was weak and cracking when she called the student-counseling center. She was panicked and didn't know where to turn. She felt like her dreams for her future had died, like a bad car-wreck right in front of her. The pain was searing, and she could barely stand up straight because her stomach hurt so badly.

She sobbed into her pillow until the counseling center called her back and asked her to come in immediately for an emergency session. After washing the tears and some of the redness off her face, her walk to campus seemed endless, because her mind was foggy, and her head was dizzy.

The counselor conducted a suicidal risk assessment, and carefully asked about Jenae's reason for being there. Jenae's slobbering description of breaking up with her boyfriend half a world away made the counselors face turn from empathy to disappointment. The therapist looked down, shook her head, closed the file, and announced that their fifty-minute session was over. Jenae felt stupid that she was in a state of emotional despair and nobody had died, or had a new cancer diagnosis. The walk back home in the fresh air changed her mood more than talking to a stranger about her feelings.

Outside her apartment her neighbor, Joe, was putting his tennis racket back in its case on the front steps.

"Hey neighbor, I haven't seen you much. Where've you been?" Joe asked Jenae.

"I was just up on campus. Oh, I was in New Zealand for a month not too long ago."

"That's exciting. Is everything OK? Joe noticed the blotches around Jenae's eyes."

"I just broke up with my boyfriend. On his birthday," Jenae said through her tears.

"Well, that sucks balls," Joe said in his Wisconsin accent and put his arm over her shoulder and gave her a side hug. Jenae leaned her head against his arm and wiped away her tears.

"That means you can hang out with us more! We're going to the dive bar down the street to watch the World Series tonight. Come with us. It's my roommate and a few classmates; I think you might know them."

The last thing Jenae wanted was to go out in public; she wanted to close the blinds and go to bed and pull the covers over her head. But for some reason she said "sure". The bar was filled to capacity with Giants and Oakland A fans because it was a monumental battle in the Bay: The first time Oakland and San Francisco MLB teams met in the World Series. Joe's friends had gone early to secure the biggest booth and get started drinking Jägermeister shots at happy hour prices. Jenae knew most everyone there from classes, including Joe's girlfriend. They were a perfect match. Jenae was glad that Joe was being a good friend and didn't want anything more from her.

Chapter 23

Rumblings

October 17th, 1989, friends of Jenae gathered at her apartment to watch the third game of the World Series before class started that evening. Joe and his girlfriend had tickets to the game and left for Candlestick Stadium at about noon.

Three of the friends were group project partners, and Jenae didn't care about baseball, but wanted to finish out the project that was due in class at 7 PM. Two had arrived at 4:30 PM and started formulating a graphic display of statistics on Jenae's antiquated computer. She had extra floppy discs for storage, but they would have to print copies of the project at the library before class started. Zeki was the fourth member of the group, and he was late because he lived in Marin County and had an internship with a big company during the day. Plus, he was Turkish and knew nothing about American baseball, nor did he care.

The classmates gathered on the peach couch in the living room, and Jenae sat on the floor facing them and placed papers on the coffee table to sort out the information. Al Michaels did the pre-game broadcast and gave statistics of each teams' players. The Oakland Athletics won the first two games in the Series already, and footage from a blimp overhead the stadium showed the perfect seventy-degree weather on an Indian-Summer day in the bay area. The game was on the San Francisco side, but the city of Oakland could be seen in the long shot of the bay, just past boats lingering on the water outside the stadium.

Jenae had started cooking chicken breasts in a frying pan, and she was going to feed her classmates chicken sandwiches and salad to keep them interested in finishing the project. She made a pitcher of unsweetened iced tea, which was becoming her favorite beverage after drinking so much tea in New Zealand; caffeine without the fizz. As she placed the plate of salad down on the coffee table, it moved, and Jenae stumbled when the floor below her feet began to judder up and down rapidly like a jackhammer.

The classmates' eyes widened and in unison, they yelled, "EARTHQUAKE!" They all knew what to do and moved to an area below a big beam that separated the kitchen and the living room and far away from the windows. Jenae held onto the wall and the others steadied themselves by holding on to each other. After the juddering stopped, a rolling action kicked in and smoothed out as the waves of the earth continued for just sixty seconds. It felt like thirty minutes to Jenae. She had been in an earthquake a few months earlier that destroyed the community hospital where she worked for extra money. But that was just a 4.2 magnitude; the hospital structure crumbled because it was ancient and not built to withstand earthquakes. Most other buildings barely felt the movements.

Jenae knew that this earthquake was much larger. Just as the ground settled, another rumbling hit that seemed the same as the first quake. They didn't know if it was an aftershock or if a bigger one was on the way.

As soon as the first quake hit, all the power shut off. The TV was black, the stovetop cooking the chicken went cold, and the refrigerator fell silent. Jenae picked up the phone receiver and heard no dial tone. The sun was setting, and they could hear dogs barking; sirens on fire trucks and police cars sped past the front of the apartment building as the group wandered outside in a daze. People from the neighborhood stood out in the streets just in case a building was to collapse. A large water main at the top of the street by the REC center broke, and a stream of water washed down the street in front of them. At the bottom of the hill, the local bodega caught Jenae's eyes, and the group walked down the block to get batteries and food. They didn't know how long power would be out and smelled gas halfway there. They weren't sure where the safest place was during an earthquake.

The bodega was dark, but the shopkeeper sat inside on a stool with the door propped open for air. He'd been watching the game on a small six-inch black and white TV with big rabbit ears. He didn't have power to open his cash register, but he had a manual card reader that took imprints with carbon paper, and Jenae had her credit card. They bought the last pack of AA batteries, along with drinks and snacks. They grabbed random items like beef jerky and sour candies when a stream of neighbors entered the store. The storekeeper got scared and shooed them all away because he didn't like the panicky energy. Jenae's group made it out with a few bags of sundries before he threw everyone out.

They walked in the middle of the main street as they headed back up the hill because no cars were driving on the roads; emergency vehicles passed by infrequently, and most had left the neighborhood for more urgent needs.

The view over the Marina District could have competed with scenes from war in Beirut or Armageddon. Helicopters hovered over buildings on fire. Red and yellow flames and black smoke were visible from the hill where Jenae and her friends stood. Dogs ran aimlessly through the streets, trying to get away from the aftershocks that followed. Most tremblers were only minutes apart, but none was as big at the first rumble.

Jenae's crew sat on the curb of the street until after dark and decided that her building was safe because it didn't have any visible damage. It was built on solid ground, not like the Marina District. She was weirdly thankful that her apartment had been swatted, and she was forced to move out. Her building in the Marina may have collapsed or caught fire or both and her mind couldn't comprehend the horror that was happening while she was relatively safe on solid rock.

Jenae found two candles, one from her bathroom and one from Paulina's bedside table. Matches were in the kitchen drawer next to the stove.

Soon it was pitch black and more students wandered into her apartment. Jenae opened the freezer, pulled every popsicle and ice cream bar out, and passed them to her friends.

As they sat in the candlelight licking the melting desserts off their fingers and hands, they heard someone calling out.

"Hello! Jenae?" Jenae walked slowly and kept a hand on a wall or piece of furniture along the way to her open door to the hallway.

"Is that you, Zeki?"

"Yes. Which floor are you on?"

"The second one. Follow my voice. We have a full house, but it's a rocking earthquake party," Jenae tried to stay lighthearted.

"I'm glad I found you. I had your address, but couldn't find it; I was going off of memory," Zeki said.

"You're a little late to work on the project, but good news! Classes are cancelled anyway. I guess we have bigger things to worry about," Jenae said.

"I went to campus first because I was so late from blocked streets, and I drove in circles trying to get here. Campus was closed down. They were taking care of campus residents, but that was it," Zeki said.

"You must have made it over the Golden Gate Bridge ahead of the earthquake, huh."

"NO! I was driving on the bridge when it hit, and I thought I had a flat tire and then two flat tires. And then the bridge started swaying back and forth. It was scary, but really cool now that I'm safe and not floating face down in the bay," Zeki said.

"What did you see?" Jenae asked.

"I got a good view of the Marina and burning buildings. The radio said that those buildings collapsed because the neighborhood was built on reclaimed land. They dredged mud and rocks out of the bay to create that beautiful flat space, but it just turned to jelly when the ground shook," Zeki said.

"It sounds like everything is shut down. No power, no gas, no water, no phone. I wonder if anyone outside of San Francisco knows that we had an earthquake?"

"Well, you all are welcome to stay overnight. I have extra blankets and pillows if you don't mind sleeping on the couch and the floor. I don't know where Paulina is, so you can use her room too until she comes back," Jenae said.

The group tried to keep their spirits up by playing games and imitating each other's mannerisms and acting out 'guess that professor.' But every time an aftershock came, they stopped, braced, and just looked around at one another in the dim light. When the trembling stopped, there was a collective laugh . . . until the next one, and the next one, throughout the evening.

Paulina wandered into the apartment before 10PM; she had walked home from her office downtown. No buses nor any other public transport was running. She looked scared and dirty, but it was nothing compared to what she saw on the walk home. Building facades had fallen on pedestrians walking on sidewalks and the smell of gas was everywhere. She thought the street would blow up underneath her feet with every step she took.

After getting a juice out of the refrigerator, she tiptoed over the guests lying on the living room floor and found a transistor radio in the bottom drawer of her clothes dresser. She had more candles stashed next to it. Her mom had made an emergency kit when she moved into the apartment because earthquakes had always been in their vernacular.

"Jenae, do you happen to have any extra batteries?" Paulina asked. Jenae was proud that she had purchased batteries at the bodega earlier that night and presented them to a Paulina with relief that she would finally be able to hear what was going on around her.

According to the reports, the Marina was still burning, and the Bay Bridge had collapsed. People were trapped in both areas, and many were assumed dead. The shock of the event kept everyone calm, but once Jenae laid down in bed at midnight to sleep, she woke to another trembler that shook her bed violently. Anxiety took over because she felt vulnerable and forgotten. She wondered if any of her family knew that she was in a real-life nightmare. She was sure that Neve hadn't heard about it all the way around the world.

By sunup, all of her visitors had vacated the apartment. Jenae and Paulina sat on the peach couch staring at the black TV screen. They ate individually packaged cookies and drank tea from the night before.

Paulina was stunned; she had lived in the Bay Area her whole life (except for college) and had never experienced a big earthquake before.

"My mom was right . . . again. Thank goodness she packed an emergency bag for me. I hope she and my dad are all right."

"I'm sure they're fine. Phones should work again soon. I'm feeling guilty because as a nurse, I'm supposed to report to the hospital in case of mass casualties. But I have no communication, and I don't have the mental energy or physical strength to work. I could walk over there, but I feel like I would collapse before I got up the hill," Jenae said.

"Don't worry about it. The radio says that there are fewer injuries than would be expected. Unfortunately, that probably means lots of people died. Just call them when the phones work again and go from there," Paulina said. Jenae never thought of Paulina as levelheaded until this crisis hit. She was younger, but much wiser than first impressions.

The roommates got dressed and wandered into the streets and walked up the big hill to the university to get a better look of the neighborhood. From Lone Mountain, they had a clear 360-degree view of the city from the ocean to the bay.

The Marina was still burning, and Jenae bowed her head to pray for the people still trapped and for the souls of those who didn't make it. She also guiltily gave thanks that she was safe and wasn't part of the worst of the disaster.

As she and Paulina walked down the grand staircase, they came upon three young undergraduate girls huddled together and sobbing. One of their friends had been killed on the Bay Bridge.

"It's not fair! We love her so much; her family loves her, and now she's gone," one of the girls cried out as they hugged each other. Jenae felt their anguish deeply, and she said another prayer of healing for them as she quietly walked by.

Chapter 24

Outside Looking In

Neve heard about the 7.4 earthquake on the San Andreas fault line almost instantaneously with the rest of the world because it was caught on live television covering the World Series. His heart sunk and he prayed that Jenae was all right. He immediately dialed her phone number but got a busy signal every time he dialed on the hour. Sky News had coverage of the rescues from the area's most hard hit by the destruction. He recognized Jenae's old apartment in the Marina District where he spent his last night in San Francisco. It was still standing, but just down the street a complete building was flattened rubble, and fire leapt out of an intersection of a main road. Pete, Hamish, and Tee all called Helen's number to check on Neve and to see if he had any more information about Jenae and her safety. With each conversation, he felt more guilt about breaking up with her. Only Hamish was aware of their change in relationship status.

Jenae's parents tried frantically calling her number but got the same busy tone. Her mom assured the neighbors who called to check on Jenae, that she was probably OK. "She always lands on her feet."

Sandy stayed up all night watching the coverage from the East Coast. She caught glimpses of her studio apartment building half collapsed and was grateful that she was far away; and that her expensive BMW was parked in Jenae's garage. Her phone calls met a busy tone, too.

<hr>

Twenty-four hours after the quake occurred, Logan threw some supplies into the back of his truck and headed over to Jenae's apartment. His brain was whirling with how he could turn this crisis into an opportunity to make Jenae love him. Then he could live happily ever after. He had water bottles, a flashlight, extra batteries, trail mix, cheese, semi-stale crackers, and a bottle of white wine. The main door to the entrance of the apartment remained propped open with the power out. Jenae was home alone because Paulina caught a ride to her parent's home with a friend. A knock on the door surprised Jenae; she thought it might be the Super checking out the condition of the apartments. She opened the door to find Logan standing with both arms full, holding brown paper grocery bags.

"You survived! I would've called first, but you know the phones aren't working. I brought you some supplies just in case. I had extra stuff lying around my place," Logan said to Jenae.

"Wow! Hi! Come on in. You didn't have to do that for me."

"Here, I'll set these down on the kitchen table, and I still have a case of water bottles for you that I need to get from my truck," Logan said.

"Thanks! I'll come and help," Jenae said.

She scampered down the staircase behind Logan and closed the back door of his truck after he grabbed the case of bottled water with both hands and steadied it on his soft pudgy belly.

"I hope you don't think that I'm intruding. I just wanted to help, and I thought of you," Logan said.

"Your donations are greatly appreciated. I had a house full of people here last night; now they're all gone along with my food. So, thanks," Jenae said.

"I brought the wine because I thought you may need to wind down and take the edge off. What a disaster!"

"It's such a tragedy; I could use a drink. Should we open it even though it isn't chilled? Jenae asked.

"Sure, I'd like to have a glass with you. There's cheese and crackers, too. You open the wine and I'll cut the cheese."

"Did you just say cut the cheese?" Jenae laughed.

Logan and Jenae talked on the peach couch for a few hours until it became completely dark in the apartment. Her candles were almost out of wax.

"You know what? I better let you go. I'm starting to get a headache, and I should probably lie down, maybe the wine has gone to my head. It's been a tough 24 hours," Jenae said.

"Sure, I'd better check in with work anyway. Get some rest." Logan waved as he walked down the stairs.

"Bye! Thanks again. See you later!"

Walking up the sidewalk at the same time was Joe and his girlfriend. They had just made it home from Candlestick Park. They were worn out and looked like they hadn't slept.

"How was the game?" Jenae snickered in poor humor.

"It was more than we bargained for," Joe retorted.

"I'm glad you both are OK. How'd you get back? Where'd you stay last night?"

"We slept at the stadium. Well, in the parking lot of the stadium, in my car," Joe said.

"We all just car camped until roads opened up again. This morning, we went to my apartment to check on my roommates," Joe's girlfriend chimed in.

"That was a nightmare. Her roommates were freaked out, and then we got stuck in the neighborhood." Joe was gassed and ready to hit his pillow and prayed that this was all a big nightmare that would go away in the morning.

As the couple stumbled up the stairs in the dark, Jenae opened the door to the garage underneath the apartment building to check on Sandy's BMW. It was safe and sound and not going anywhere until the power got turned back on because the electric garage door was dead like everything else.

Jenae was stuck and lonely, but at least she wasn't dead. If only she could have been stuck with Neve; it would have been a very different story.

⸺◦⸺

Sleep was more peaceful the night after the initial earthquake; Jenae only woke twice with the shaking of her bed from aftershocks. In the morning, the refrigerator started humming again and the clock radio beside her bed flashed red illuminated numbers at her.

A huge relief rolled over her shoulders when she realized that life might get back to normal again. She picked up the phone receiver over and over again hoping to hear a dial tone, but it remained silent. She turned on the TV for the first time since power was cut from the quake and was surprised to see constant coverage of the Bay Area. A bigheaded news reporter talked into a fuzzy microphone as he pointed to the smashed-up Bay Bridge behind him. Then the national station cut to a blonde-haired woman standing next to a fire truck with smoking buildings behind her. They talked about the geological event being witnessed by millions around the world because it happened at 5:04 PM, before the opening inning of a World Series baseball game.

After watching the coverage for a few hours, she felt grateful and overwhelmed. At least she knew her family was aware of the event, even though she couldn't communicate with them.

Her power was back on, she got some REM sleep, and had enough supplies to last her for a few days, but she was already stir crazy. The BMW was lonely, too, and Jenae hadn't gotten to drive it yet. The garage door could open since the power was back on, and Jenae decided to go on a quick drive to drop by the medical center and to see damages around the city firsthand.

Streets had dried up from the water main break because the sun was shining with bluebird skies. Jenae pressed the button on the ceiling of the Beemer to open the sunroof. As she backed out of the garage, sunlight streamed in warming her head and shoulders. She unrolled the driver's side window and felt a calming cool breeze on her face as she picked up speed.

Other than helicopters flying overhead, the streets were peaceful. Jenae drove past the university where barricades were placed at the entrances to keep strangers and looters out of their sanctuary. Traffic lights were blinking red or yellow at every intersection. She turned right toward the park and the med center. Although she heard from the news that injuries were nominal and hospitals were able to handle the load, she needed to assuage her guilt of not checking in.

She parked in the circle drive in the loading zone so she wouldn't have to pay for the garage. Security would most likely think the BMW belonged to a doctor who needed to quickly swoop in to care for a patient. The nurse management office was pleased that she stopped in. Although they weren't experiencing an extra patient load from the destruction, they had a large percentage of nurses who couldn't make it to work because the Bay Bridge collapsed. Jenae signed up to work the next three days and go from there. Her guilt index lowered, and she was pleased to have a distraction from sitting at home alone waiting for classes to start up again.

Jenae tried to drive to the Marina, but too many emergency vehicles were parked in the roadway. Many residents and looky-loos wandered the streets, but Jenae didn't want to park and add to the mayhem. Pacific Heights and the Golden Gate Bridge were no worse for wear, although a local newscaster had highlighted damage to historic military barracks in the Presidio.

She avoided going downtown and stayed north to stay out of the way of rescue operations. The drive around town felt productive, but also gave Jenae a good reason to lie down for a nap when she got home. A ringing phone woke her up. She sat straight up, and her heart leapt, she didn't care who was on the line. She was connected again.

"Hello?" Jenae said.

"Jenae! Are you OK?" It was Neve with a tremble in his voice.

"Yes! I'm OK, but we've had a terrible earthquake here."

"I know! I've been worried sick about you. I've been trying to call you, but I always got a busy signal."

"You have? You are my first call to come through since it happened. I didn't think you would've heard about it."

"Jenae, it's all over the news here, and I've just been so worried about you for all these hours. I love you." Neve teared up as he felt the pain of possibly losing Jenae forever.

Jenae's heart was full and sad at the same time. She missed Neve and loved him and couldn't believe that he was the first to get through to her on the phone. Her heart was still broken from their split. They only talked for ten minutes, and Neve promised to write her a letter. She wasn't sure if they would have a future together or not.

As soon as she hung up the phone from Neve, it rang again. It was Sandy calling from Boston.

"Oh my God! I finally got through to you. Are you OK? Did your apartment survive? I assume it did since you answered the phone."

"Yes, I'm OK and my apartment's sturdy and sound. And your BMW is fine, too. Nice and safe in our garage," Jenae said.

"Thanks for telling me that. I wasn't going to ask because I didn't want to sound shallow, but it's good to know," Sandy said.

"It's a good thing that you brought it over here before you left, because your neighborhood is toast. You may want to stay on the East Coast longer if you can. Recovery is going to take a while here, and I don't know that you will be able to return to your cute apartment."

"I already changed my flight and my friends in San Jose have offered me a room at their house when I get back. It's close to my work," Sandy said.

"Let me know when you'll arrive at the airport. I can try to pick you up if I'm not working at the hospital. If not, I'll leave the keys for you under the floor mat and give you the combo to get out of the garage."

"I'm glad you are OK, Jenae. I'm going to try to find my other friends now that I know that the phones in the city are working," Sandy said in relief.

Chapter 25

Reconsideration and Magic

The call with Jenae after the earthquake stuck with Neve, even after he wrote her a long letter contemplating their breakup. He only thought about two things: flying and Jenae. Passing his instrument rating exam and getting his rating meant non-stop studying and practice in the simulator. He had difficulty getting used to wearing a helmet-hood to practice focusing on just the instruments without relying on what he saw outside of the windows: It made him concentrate on one thing and one thing only—flying and landing the plane safely.

When at home, he found himself focused on Jenae and wondered how he could be happy without her in his life and realized what he needed to do to get her back. He made a call to a therapist who could help him decipher the PTSD that he had experienced while he was in the police force. The shooting that saved a woman's life took another's life at his hands. In a sick, twisted way, he felt that he had to pay for it karmically. His life had to be ruined too, because of that tragic day.

Therapy was hard while he was in the session, but he felt lighter and had more tools in his mental health belt that he could rely on afterward. It almost felt like he did as a kid after he went to confession in the Catholic Church. Talking to the priest behind a mesh wall about the sins of a young boy seemed like the end of the world. Disrespecting his mother and father were at the top of the list, along with missing Sunday Masses and Holy Days of Obligation. Prayers in the pew after confession usually included a few Hail Mary's and an Our Father, and Neve felt better about himself; like a weight had been taken off his shoulders. He wanted to do and be better but hadn't returned to church after the shooting.

<hr>

Jenae kept her head in the books to finish out the broken semester and worked at the hospital the rest of the time. They were always short nurses, and she was willing to float to other units away from her cardiovascular floor to help out.

On a day shift on the medical unit, she had a patient assigned to her who she knew from her grad school classes. He was a slight young man, about her age, with sandy hair and big brown eyes. Jenae was surprised to see him in the hospital and asked to switch patients with another nurse for ethical reasons before she found out too much about his case. She had seen from his diagnosis that he had cancer and Kaposi sarcoma. He had been admitted for dehydration due to cancer treatments on his gastrointestinal tract. Jenae had no idea that he had AIDs until the patient sat down with her in the solarium waiting room and laid it all out for her. He had lesions, big and small, on his face and neck and dark circles under his eyes. He was frequently admitted to the hospital, especially as his condition worsened. He told Jenae that his goal was to graduate with his MBA before he died. He only had one more spring semester, and they could graduate together.

Time moved slower than usual on that day because Jenae almost wanted it to. Her friend was dying, and she had no idea he was even sick before that morning. He was her age. He was at the end of his life, and she had her whole future ahead of her. He was kind, measured, and graceful, she knew how this was going to go. She had taken care of many AID's patients during their final hours in Dallas and in San Francisco. At the small community hospital, young men had family members or significant others by their side as they drew their last breath. But Jenae's friend didn't have a boyfriend, and he was too scared to tell his family at home in South Carolina.

⚬

In the final month of the semester, finance class wasn't as serious as the instructor wanted it to seem. Jenae and her soft-spoken friend from the hospital laughed and had fun as much as possible, even if it was at the stuffy professor's expense.

Letters from Neve came twice a week, and he mostly wrote about aviation, stock investments, and mentioned just once that he had started therapy. Talking once a week to his therapist, allowed Neve to explore negative experiences in his childhood and throughout his time on the SWAT team, while working in the police department. He wanted Jenae to come back to New Zealand for her break in December and spend Christmas with him. He was confident that he would pass his instrument ratings class by then and wouldn't be as stressed out. He hoped that they could reconcile and make another go of it. He offered to buy her airline ticket if she agreed.

Jenae's mind and time was occupied with school, work, and her friends. Now that Neve was gone, she had more time to let loose and experience the city. Sandy invited Jenae to a girlfriend group dinner with her tech friends.

"How are you managing without Neve? Are you over him yet?" Sandy asked.

"I don't know what I feel. It's a relief that he's doing what he's passionate about, but I do miss him. I'm not sure if we'll get back together though," Jenae said.

"I know how to clear your mind; let's all go to Las Vegas for a weekend! Before the holidays kick in," Sandy said.

"What? It's been a while since I've been there. In fact, the last time, I was there with Neve," Jenae said.

"Let's have a girl's weekend. Everyone at this table has to go. Next weekend. Southwest Airlines has tickets for dirt-cheap right now, and I have points on my credit card for a hotel room. Everybody in?"

"Sure, why not," Jenae resigned. The two other ladies were hyped on their vodka-tonics and were ready to live it up, too.

Professors at school were ultra lenient on assignments since the earthquake. Jenae worked ahead to finish her papers so that she could put in her work hours during the week in preparation for the girl's trip to Vegas. Viva Las Vegas

⸻◦○◦⸻

Sandy and the crew from San Francisco deplaned from their nineteen-dollar flight, and walked to the taxi area of the airport to find a ride to the Strip. Two men from Louisiana chatted up Sandy and offered the entire girl crew a ride to their hotel in a hired limousine that was sent by their clients. They were there for work and seemed to be attorneys for a dubious organization. Jenae was suspicious that the mafia may be involved somehow. The attorneys had a table reserved at the Siegfried and Roy Magic Show that night and invited the four ladies to fill up the six-seat booth with them.

"Let me have your last name, and I can leave the extra tickets at the concierge at your hotel for you ladies," the mobster said.

"I don't know what we've got planned so, don't worry about it," Sandy said.

"They'll go to waste, anyway; come if you can. They will be waiting for you. The show starts at nine. We'll see you there, or maybe not. Either way, have a great weekend."

The girls checked into their double-queen hotel room with a big picture window that looked over the Strip. They had no plans except for gambling and trying to get tickets to the male strip show review. None of the girls were big gamblers, but enjoyed the shows and free drinks when they sat at slot machines and plugged quarters in for the thrill of winning a few more than they put in. They ate dinner at a famous chef's restaurant with an open kitchen where they watched the cooks stir pasta with vegetables in single serving frying pans. The flames licked up to the copper hood.

Sandy mentioned the magic show tickets when dessert was served, and she was surprised by the other girls' response.

"Of course we should go. Free tickets?"

"What could those guys do to us? It's four against two, and they looked pretty feeble."

It was a consensus; the girls finished dinner and picked up the tickets left for them at the concierge desk. The Louisiana Lawyers' expressions couldn't hide their surprise and excitement when four hot, young ladies walked up to their table and sat down. They both stood up to greet them and to give them the best seats in the semi-circle red velvet padded booth. They ordered rounds of drinks for the table and a bottle of champagne to share. They were free spenders because it was all going to be expensed to their client. The show was entertaining with big lions and tigers and fancy dressed trainers from Germany. Jenae was confused as what the disappearing and reappearing thrill was all about. From her vantage point, she could clearly see look-a-likes appearing for Siegfried and Roy. The disguises were good from far away, but not great from her angle.

Gambling at the craps table was Sandy's thing. She knew all the rules because her father had a craps table in their game room growing up. Jenae and the others watched as the dice rolled to the end of the well and the players staggered around it and cheered or booed. Jenae got selected by a boisterous man in polyester pants to take his turn at rolling the dice. She blew on the dice every time before she threw them. The players were in sync with her rolls and cheered more than they booed.

The ladies didn't mind sharing beds after staying out until 3:30 AM. Oxygen pumped into the casino kept patrons awake and energized to keep gambling. By noon, the ladies found a buffet restaurant and played Keno from the table as they ate and watched the numbers come up over shrimp cocktail and prime rib. Jenae played numbers that Paulina had given her along with a ten-dollar bill. Paulina got the best return on her bet by winning fifty bucks.

During the afternoon, they hung out by the pool and caught some rays and ZZZ's to prepare for their big night. Jenae found tickets to the early performance of Australia's Thunder Down Under Male review.

Their seats were in the first row of the balcony, close enough to see all the glistening muscles, but too far away to be embarrassed by being pulled up on stage. They whooped and hollered when the cast of shirtless men in jeans, boots, and belts filled the stage and gyrated in unison. The seducers changed costumes and pulled young women with birthday and bachelorette sashes up on stage. Ladies covered their mouths when the half-naked men simulated sexual acts with only a few inches between them. Their eyes widened, and they screamed with joy with each pelvic thrust.

A walk down the famous neon-illuminated strip was filled with tourists and promoters handing pamphlets out for discounts to a local strip club or a better buffet. Sandy and Jenae got really good at saying "no thank you" before a leaflet was flashed in front of their faces. The other girls ignored them completely. By the end of the night, they had offers to do lines of cocaine with some screenwriters from LA and to go to a party off the strip at a 'producer's mansion.' Red flags went off in all of their minds preventing certain regret.

Chapter 26

Angel and Demons

Logan called Jenae several times in his manic state, and when she didn't return his calls, he became more and more desperate for her attention. Jenae called him back when she returned from her girl's trip in Vegas, and he invited her to go on a bike ride on Angel Island. He told her he wanted to discuss Neve's visa—he had very important news. The fresh air on one last ferry ride to Angel Island would do her good before finals started.

Logan picked her up in his truck and placed her blue bike in the back with his.

"Hey beautiful! How was your trip to Vegas with the girls?" Logan asked with a strained smile on his face.

"Oh, it was fun, and you are too kind. You can call me Jenae."

"Sorry, it just slipped. I think you're gorgeous if you haven't figured that out yet," Logan said.

Jenae changed the subject, "It looks like we picked a great day to get out on the water, it's calm and sunny."

They reached the ferry launch and walked their bikes over the plank to the boat. Several other adventurers, including small children, rolled their trail bikes into the designated rack next to theirs.

"Should we go to the front of the boat? I think the view will be spectacular from up there," Logan suggested.

The water was choppy as they passed by Alcatraz Island, and seagulls followed the boat waiting for snacks to be thrown to them by eager tourists. The Golden Gate Bridge was a striking orange against the light blue sky. Jenae hadn't realized the expansive height and length of the bridge until she saw it from the water surface on a clear day. She wondered if a plane could fly underneath it. Logan clearly understood why jumpers were always successful committing suicide. Hitting the water from that height would be like smashing onto concrete. The cold water below would take away any breath left in a jumper's body.

After the ferry safely docked on Angel Island, the duo walked their bikes to a large wooden sign that showed all the walking and riding trails. Jenae placed her helmet on her head and clipped the buckle under her chin. She then took a swig of water from the plastic bottle pinched in the holder on her bike. Logan didn't have a helmet or a water bottle.

As they rode up and down dusty trails on the island, Jenae was nervous to bring up her breakup with Neve to Logan because she still wanted to get his visa straightened out, and she thought they could mend their relationship. She still loved

Neve but was worried about their future. They stopped at an overlook to cool off and catch their breaths.

"How is Neville handling being away from you? New Zealand is really far away," Logan said.

"To be honest, he broke up with me after my visit over the summer, but we are communicating again. I'm going back to visit him over Christmas to see if we can work things out."

"Why did he do that?"

"I think he got frustrated with the situation and wanted to concentrate on flying," Jenae said.

"I've been in that situation. My fiancée couldn't handle my sporadic traveling schedule either."

"That's too bad, it must have been difficult to lose your true love," Jenae said.

"I thought she was my forever person, but if she hadn't left me, I would have never found you."

"What do you mean?" Jenae asked with a furrowed brow.

"She and I broke up a few months before I got assigned to watch your place in Hawaii last summer."

"What exactly did you observe while you watched our condo in Hawaii?" Jenae asked.

"It was very exciting, even though you were with a different guy. I wished I was there with you instead of just watching," Logan said.

"You watched me have sex with Neve from the other building?"

"Oh yeah. But don't blame the FBI, you left your curtains open. It was like you wanted me to watch. Like I said, it was really exciting for me," Logan said.

Jenae's blood began to boil as she looked away to the cityscape of San Francisco and then down to her hands as she picked at a callus that had built up from grabbing onto the handlebars.

"Don't worry. I don't hold it against you. You are my girlfriend now. I'll treat you like a queen and protect you from all harm. You know there are a lot of sickos in this world." Logan looked at her side-eyed.

Jenae looked around for any bikers or hikers that could help her if she got into trouble. She was scared that she was isolated on an island with no phones and a crazy person. *What if they missed the last ferry back to the city?* Jenae thought.

This guy could be a psychopath just like Neve said.

"What's wrong sweetheart? You look a little pale," Logan said.

"Logan, we are not an item. I think you're confused," Jenae said.

"Oh, I'd say we have a strong relationship. Sure, we haven't kissed or anything, but we are connected in the heart. Only your true boyfriend would help you move and take you out to dinner and musicals. Who checked on you after the earthquake and brought you water and supplies? We shared that romantic evening with a bottle of wine, remember, darling?"

"But I don't like you like that. You said that you were working on Neve's visa!"

Logan laughed and gave an outward sigh.

"Yeah, about that. I did check with my buddy at immigration and asked him to pull the visa process on Neville. The guy owed me a favor—I knew that Neville wasn't the right guy for you. Not after how he humiliated me in Hawaii."

"So, you were behind him having to leave the country?"

"You could say that, sweetheart. I needed for you to see how much I cared about you without him around," Logan said.

Jenae's eyes filled with tears. She was terrified and sad that she had ruined Neve's dream.

"How did you find me back on the mainland?"

"I'm not going to lie, that took a lot of resources . . . and you like the dolphin and heart figurine bracelet, don't you?"

"You left that in my bag? What's in it? A creepy guy chased me around the hospital when I wore that to work one night."

"I just had a little tracking bug placed in the heart charm. I wanted to keep track of you so that we could meet again. I promised that street criminal some heroin if he would check on you and give you a little scare," Logan said with an evil grin.

"What about the swatting at my apartment in the Marina, were you behind that, too?" Jenae asked.

"I knew you'd be at work, so it was just your snotty roommate that got scared on that mission. An anonymous caller from Merced made that threat," Logan said.

Jenae's heart raced in her chest as her eyes darted back and forth trying to figure out her best escape route. She saw a ferry approaching the island and wanted to make a break for it.

Jenae had a bird's-eye view from the peak of Angel Island. She wiped her clammy hands on her bike pants as she formulated a plan to make it to the ferry chugging straight for the dock. *Slow down, if the boat doesn't slow its wake, I'm in big trouble.* Jenae thought.

"Let's check out this path." Jenae didn't look Logan in the eyes; she stood up on her pedals and took off downhill as fast as she could. Logan hesitated as she darted down the hill. He turned his bike around and adjusted his feet and straddled the saddle. "Hey! Wait for me!"

Jenae didn't turn around; she concentrated on every bump in the path to avoid rocks and to make the turns as quickly as she could.

Logan was far behind and as he started to pick up speed, he lost control, launched off the trail, and landed in a bristly bush next to a pine tree. Logan's head hit a small stone hidden in the tall grass when he fell. His head spun and he saw stars when he got his bell rung.

Jenae heard his yelp, and she turned around to see how much lead she had on him. She didn't see him lying in the grass below the trail. Jenae felt relieved and breathed easier knowing she could get make the 2:10 ferry to Tiburon. As she boarded and watched the ferry plank lifted without Logan on the boat, she sunk to the ground with bent knees. She hung on the side rail and cranked her neck to watch for him until the island became a big rock in the bay and the trees became a shadowy green mass.

Even if he could make the last ferry of the day to Tiburon, he would miss the boat back to the city at 3:15.

Jenae's mind raced as she processed what Logan had just confessed to her. *He really is a crazy stalker. There are no limits to what he would do to me or Neve.*

She boarded the last ferry back to the city, and Jenae finally sat down on a metal bench to catch her breath.

Logan lost consciousness for a few minutes and when he came to, he watched Jenae's ferry pull away from the dock on Angel Island. When he dragged his bike back to upright position, he noticed that his chain had fallen off. He tried to get it back in place but had to walk the bike to the docking area instead because his shaking hands had lost coordination.

The last ferry back to Tiburon pulled up to the dock just after Logan stumbled to the embarkment area. He wiped his face and with his T-shirt and saw a pink streak from his bloodied forehead on it. A woman next to him touched his back and leaned in. "Are you OK?"

Logan tilted his head up and squinted as he looked into the woman's eyes, "I'll be fine, thanks." As he looked into the distance, he watched the ferry from Tiburon back to the city chug by.

Jenae looked back to Angel Island from the back of that ferry and wondered how big of a head start she had on Logan.

Logan stood up and stumbled. He touched his forehead again and grimaced. The woman handed him a tissue to dab the blood mixed with dirty sweat. He felt dizzy again as he looked up to see the wake of Jenae's boat chugging back to the city.

<hr>

Jenae knew the quickest way home on her bike was to avoid the big hills by riding along the shoreline. She followed the bay as best she could and prayed that Logan wouldn't catch up to her. He truly was a psychopathic stalker, just like Neve warned her. The only thing she wanted to do was call Neve and get a sense of security back.

"Neve, It's me, Jenae. I'm so sorry that I didn't listen to you. You're a hundred percent right; Logan is a really sick man and a bad dude! He's the reason why you lost your visa status here. He wasn't helping us; he wanted you gone so he could have me in his own creepy head. I'm so sorry. I love you so much!" Jenae said to the recording on the answering machine. She didn't care if Helen heard it first.

<hr>

Logan lost consciousness on the ferry ride to Tiburon. He was loaded into an ambulance and remembered seeing the orange spires and suspension cables of the Golden Gate bridge flashing in the back window of the rig as paramedics pumped up a blood pressure cuff on his arm and shined tiny lights in his eyes.

An EMT started an IV in his arm and placed sticky tabs on his chest that were connected to a machine that showed his heart rhythm. It beeped at a steady pace. He was alive but scared that he told Jenae too much. She didn't understand how much love he had for her. Logan knew that they were meant to be together; they were soul mates.

Logan passed out again, but roused by the sound of the sirens blaring from the ambulance and the EMT shaking his shoulder. They arrived at the medical center where Jenae worked. He fantasized that she would be in the emergency room dressed in her scrubs, demanding to take care of 'the greatest love of her life.' Logan was admitted to the ICU, and Jenae was nowhere to be seen.

⸺◆⸺

Jenae stood in her shower and let the warm spray wash away her salty sheen. She didn't know what to do next and didn't know if Logan was still stuck on Angel Island with his demons, or if he was outside her front door plotting his next move. Paulina came home as Jenae talked on the phone with Sandy.

"You need to get the hell out of the city before Logan finds you again," Sandy advised strongly.

Paulina, on the other hand, wanted her to wait it out and see if he showed up again. Paulina selfishly and understandably didn't want to be alone in the apartment if he came back. Jenae decided to side with Paulina. The two of them could buddy up coming and going from the apartment, and Jenae didn't have transportation to do anything else. Jenae had finals coming up and her plan was to hole up in the library that was only accessible by students and faculty.

Chapter 27

Crazy Daze

Psychopaths were not foreign in Jenae's past. She thought back to two who affected her life at a young age.

Teddy Bera was a neighbor boy who lived a few streets over from her childhood home. He was an only child who was adopted by an older couple and was one year older than Jenae and one year younger than her sister. He had recently gone through puberty and wore a black baby-hair mustache—his parents hadn't taught him how to shave yet.

Jenae lived in a sprawling house; it was an old home with a big new addition built on. Large picture windows in a cathedral arched great room gave a feeling of outdoor living. Likewise, a full wall of sliding glass doors in the dining room created a wilderness view of their quiet wooded five-acre property. No curtains were needed, because the house couldn't be seen from the street or from any neighbors.

One summer night, Jenae's dad was out of town with her older brothers at an AAU swim meet. Her mother and younger twin brothers slept in rooms in the new addition while Jenae and her sister shared a room at the very back of the original house, far away from the others.

At 1:13 AM, Jenae's thirteen-year-old sister awoke and saw a boy at their clothes dresser opening and closing drawers. Brass handles on the sturdy Ethan Allen piece of furniture hung down and swung back and forth as the hooded stranger released them. Clinking sounds against lacquered oak drawers awakened her sister and she sat up in bed to focus on what was really happening. She thought, 'am I dreaming?'

Her heart pounded, and her hands were clammy when she screamed bloody murder. The boy turned to look at her and ran out of their room with her sister in chase through the long ambling house. He exited the way he came in: through the dining room's open sliding glass door. He disappeared into the wooded property, but her sister knew exactly who he was when he showed his face—Teddy Bera.

Jenae awoke and saw the shadowy figure duck his head and run out of the room with her sister on his heels. She had missed most of the action, but ran after both of them in support. Jenae shut the sliding glass door and locked it. The commotion aroused their mother, who ran down the main staircase to come to the aide of her daughters.

"What's happening?" Mother asked.

"Teddy Bera was in our room going through our drawers!" her sister cried hysterically.

"Jeez us! Are you OK? Did he touch you? Are you sure he left the house?"

"Yes, we both saw him run out here and through the trees," Jenae said.

Mother paced back and forth from the kitchen to the dining room, not sure what to do next. She took deep breaths with her head down and her hands on her knees, trying not to pass out.

After she gained composure, she looked up the phone number for the police department in the city directory white pages. She picked up the receiver and dialed each number carefully with her shaking fingers. When the dispatcher answered, she described the situation with a trembling voice and emphasized that her husband and older male sons were out of town. She was vulnerable. As soon as she hung up, she grabbed both daughters and hugged them.

"Come on girls, let's sit in my bathroom together until the police arrive."

Jenae wasn't as shook up as her sister because she'd only caught the tail end of the break in. Her adrenaline was still pumping from the chase out of the house.

Mother had them lock the bathroom door while she checked on the twins sleeping in their room down the hallway. They were quiet as a mouse and slept through it all.

Two police officers approached the front door with flashlights and red light spinning and glowing on top of their cruiser. Once Mother let them in the house to investigate, she felt safe again.

As the cops cleared each room with their guns drawn, they swiftly and confidently moved with the precision and gracefulness of a dance. They progressed methodically to the back of the house where the girls' bedroom was located and flipped the switch to turn on the overhead lights. Covers from the twin beds were disheveled and the sheets hung off touching the cream wool carpet below. A top dresser drawer was open, which revealed girls' panties and bras. One padded bra was lying on the carpet just outside of the room, along with a string of underpants like breadcrumbs that were left behind by the intruder.

For Jenae and her sister, being locked in the upstairs bathroom felt safe until they heard a knock on the door.

"Young ladies, you can come out now, the coast is clear," a man's voice said.

Her sister didn't buy it. "How do we know that you aren't Teddy trying to trick us to come out? Maybe he's done something to Mom."

"Girls, it's OK. The police have cleared the house, and nobody is in here anymore. Unlock the door please. The nice policemen want to ask you questions," Mom spoke sweetly close to the door crack.

Jenae turned the small lock in the gold-colored door handle and Mother opened the door.

The policemen interviewed the girls at the kitchen table in the room where the invader entered and exited. Sister was sure that it was Teddy, the neighbor kid, and the police promptly left for Teddy's house. The girls slept with their mother for the rest of the night in her king-sized bed with the bedroom door locked.

Jenae learned to compartmentalize traumatic events at an early age, and this break-in didn't affect her as much as it did her sister. Her sister was the real hero and protected Jenae. Jenae was only her back up.

Crazy ways became higher stakes when a local family was massacred in their home only a few blocks away from Jenae's father's medical office. In high school, Jenae was employed as the cleaner for his office. She earned sixty dollars per month, which was good running around money for an hour of vacuuming, cleaning bathrooms, and taking out the trash five nights a week.

The first attack was a mystery and seemed random, until another and another occurred with the same modus operandi. Women were targeted and attacked by a serial killer. He broke into houses while they were out and laid in wait until the victims returned to their homes.

Life was free and easy before BTK. Hardly anyone locked their doors, and it wasn't uncommon for friends to let themselves in to other people's houses to play. After BTK, families made key chains for each of their children with keys that fit shiny new dead bolt locks on the front and back doors.

BTK, the serial killer, gave himself the moniker after writing a letter to the local paper and signing it Bind, Torture, Kill. The police had zero leads on this person and thought he might have been incarcerated, or dead, when the killings stopped.

At Jenae's house, her mom started locking the doors, but she kept the key in a decorative rock by the front door. It seemed safe enough for a family of eight, and friends and neighbors could get in if they needed to.

BTK reemerged just after Jenae started cleaning her dad's offices after dark. A woman came forward to the police after she found a note in her kitchen from the killer. He had spent the night in her basement waiting for her to return so that he could rape and kill her. He was especially angry that he had wasted his time because she didn't come home that night. Instead, she'd stayed at a friend's house. That woman lived less than a mile from Jenae's family home.

Jenae's father was shaken, and 'did some paperwork at the office while she cleaned,' for a few weeks. She felt much safer, even though the office building was always securely locked.

When it came time to go solo, Jenae tried to clean as early as possible, but with winter's schedule she often found herself racing to the front door to quickly unlock the heavy glass door that would protect her from anyone lurking in the parking lot. Carrying a large plastic bag of trash to the dumpster in the parking lot was her last task. It made Jenae pause and take deep breaths and scan the area to make sure nobody was waiting for her behind the bushes. A few nights she left the trash at the back door and told her father that she just couldn't go into the graveled parking lot all by herself. Her father acted like he was put out, but he understood, and was glad that she looked out for her own safety.

BTK was caught decades later and was found to be a sexual deviant. He dressed in women's panties and bras and had pictures of himself hanging upside down from tree branches. Jenae compartmentalized, but she also saw the pieces of the puzzle and realized that life could be a dangerous endeavor.

Chapter 28

Shifty Treats

Logan recovered from his head injury enough to be transferred out of ICU and to a bed on a medical floor. He still suffered from headaches and had memory loss, but he hadn't forgotten about Jenae, knowing that she worked on the other side of the hospital. He looked out his window hoping she would walk by. His feelings went hot and cold for her. How could she have left him there on the side of the path, he could have died. On the other hand, she probably got scared. He could get past that if she would just apologize.

She'd mentioned that Neve wanted her to come back to New Zealand for Christmas to make another go of it. *She should be finished with her finals; maybe she was working a few shifts before she went.*

***

Indeed, Jenae was cramming in three back-to-back twelve-hour shifts before her trip to New Zealand for her winter vacation. Neve had purchased her plane ticket, because he wanted her safe and out of reach from Logan—and he loved her. Jenae hadn't heard a word from Logan since leaving him stranded on Angel Island. She thought that maybe he took the hint that she wasn't interested and decided to leave her alone. She could ease her mind in just a few days when she would disappear to the other hemisphere.

Meanwhile, Logan was only a few hundred yards from her on another wing. He told his nurse that he wanted to walk the halls, and afterward, the nurse left him just a few feet away from his room to get back on his own while she answered a call button. Logan took the opportunity to wander to Jenae's unit to check if she was working that day. He peeked around a corner and saw her coming down a hallway straight for him. She would see him for sure if she turned the corner. Logan backed up and found a bathroom to duck into. He locked the door and listened outside for her to pass.

Logan's mood swung from love to hate in that moment. He heard her talking to another staff member about going back to New Zealand in a few days. "That bitch!" Logan said under his breath as her voice trailed off on the other side of the door.

He had an idea. Jenae was severely allergic to eggs, and he was going to stop her from going on that trip. Back in his room, he opened the yellow pages that he borrowed from the nurse's station. He looked up a local bakery and ordered a dozen malasada donuts filled with custard. He asked for a special filling of whipped meringue and pink sugar for six more. The more egg whites the better. He knew that Jenae loved pink things, and thought she could be enticed into splurging on a sugar binge.

The bakery rushed to fill the order and delivered it to his hospital room that day. Logan procured a magic marker from the nurse, and wrote a note on the top of the box. "Sweets for the nurses who have taken good care of me. P.S. The pink donuts are whipped cream. No egg."

Just before shift change, the unit secretary gave the nurses a heads up that a patient's family had left all of them a treat on the table in the break room, and thought it was from Jenae's patient because he said something about her going on a long vacation.

"You better grab one quick before the next shift arrives. Jenae, there are even some without egg—the pink ones."

Jenae grabbed a pink sugared malasada, wrapped it in a paper towel, and stuffed it into her backpack for later, then made final rounds on her patients. Luckily, most of them were asleep, and she got report recorded first and clocked out on time.

⊷⊷⊷◉⊷⊷⊷

The walk home in the dark seemed less scary as she picked at the donut. She was starving, because nurses only had one meal break in the middle of the day, even though they worked through lunch and dinner hours. "Yum, this is delicious. I haven't had this flavor of filling in a long time. Is it vanilla or almond?" She talked to herself as if she was talking to a friend.

As she approached her apartment, she had a coughing fit and her throat got itchy and started narrowing. Her breathing became uncomfortable, but didn't feel like a true emergency. She went straight to the kitchen and poured herself a glass of water and grabbed five 1000 mg vitamin C tablets. She washed them down quickly, because she wanted to abate any illness coming on and wanted to be one hundred percent for her month-long trip to New Zealand.

As she sat on the couch watching a sitcom on TV, she became nauseated with a pit in her stomach. She brushed it off, blamed the vitamin C, and resisted the urge to vomit, because she wanted the vitamins to stay in her system.

Her flight was in two days, and although finals and work were finished until next semester, she had errands to run. She needed a haircut, a manicure and pedicure, and to shop for gifts to take back to Neve and his family. She also wanted to buy a cute Christmas dress and something to wear for lambing on the farm with Neve's future brother-in-law. She really needed a pair of hiking boots, too.

The allergic response to the egg in the filling of the malasada donut sent Jenae to bed with a bad case of vertigo and diarrhea. She grabbed the wall and stabilized herself as she walked to the toilet multiple times throughout the night. Sleep was impossible, because the bed spun when she closed her eyes. Lying down made the dizziness worse, and she felt like she was on a boat in the middle of a storm. A headache settled in as the sun rose, and Jenae checked her medicine stash and found Tylenol and an antiemetic left over from a previous procedure. Relief came as she slept the entire day away. The anti-nausea medication had done its job—it knocked her out. She couldn't feel dizziness while she was unconscious.

Once Jenae halfway recovered from her illness, she realized that she had been suffering from food poisoning—most likely from the malasada. She felt violated because somehow it felt intentional. Her flu-like symptoms subsided, except for a touch of dizziness that kept her from her final shopping spree before leaving for New Zealand.

A shuttle service picked her up three hours before her flight was scheduled to depart from SFO. The driver was originally from Australia, and shared his experiences as an exotic pet supplier. He and his buddy camped in the outback most weekends and collected spiders and snakes and other reptiles to be sold to customers all around the world. Jenae was thankful that New Zealand didn't have any snakes or other dangerous spiders like Australia. The government was diligent about keeping foreign species out. She remembered the flight attendants at the end of her last flight there sprayed an aerosol concoction up and down the aisles of the airplane before they landed in Auckland. Passengers peeled and shoved orange segments and grapes into their mouth prior to the announcement of the preventive spray. All fresh fruits and vegetables were required to have been consumed before landing.

Aboard the massive jet, Jenae put her biggest bag in the overhead bin with the help of a willing passenger. He could see that she was struggling to maintain her balance. Once seated in her window seat, she felt at ease in the plane that would take her far, far away from Logan and back into the safety of Neve's arms. She wondered how long it would be until Neve could fly her around in a commercial jet and fantasized about his voice making announcements from the flight deck. In her last phone conversation, he was especially excited because he passed his instrument rating exams and received his certificate. He was golden from this point forward and could start getting more hours using instruments in the cockpit and not just visuals.

The physical distance between them had taken a toll on their relationship, and Logan had a devious role in that. Jenae was keenly aware that this trip would determine whether they had a future together or not.

⸺◦⸺

Neve's mood was consistently the highest it had been in years. He had a half dozen therapy sessions under his belt and dealt with childhood issues as well as his major trauma of killing a man while on duty as a cop. He started meditating twice a day and worked out after flying lessons to wind down. He was up to 450 push-ups a day. His hard work paid off and he passed all the tests that gave him his instrument rating so that he could progress in his aviation education and career.

Neve made enough money on the stock market through trading to keep him afloat and pay for Jenae's plane ticket out to see him over Christmas break—and to buy her a few big gifts. He was excited to take a vacation for himself and Jenae to the southern-most part of the South Island. 'Summer is the perfect time to go, and Jenae will love it,' He thought to himself as he looked up hotel rooms and activities from a brochure he found at the airport terminal. 'I wish I could fly us down there—someday,' Neve pondered.

•◦•

Jenae's dizziness subsided after she fell asleep on the airplane reading a boring trade magazine left in the pocket of the seat in front of her. When she woke, all she could do was think about the hell she had just came out of with Logan and the heaven she expected to find in New Zealand with Neve.

Her heart swelled with thoughts of embracing him again. She had confirmed that Neve was right all along about Logan; that he was only out to destroy Neve and their relationship. The feelings in Jenae's heart meant that Neve was exactly the person she wanted to be with: trustworthy, daring and fun. She always wanted to be with a man who wanted her—but not in the creepy way Logan wanted her. Once Neve sorted out his true feelings for her, Jenae knew that he was the kind of man that she wanted—someone who would fight for her and come after her.

Chapter 29

Kiwi Magic

Jenae remembered to walk outside to get to her next terminal after her long flight from SFO. The weather was much warmer than last time. She called Neve from the pay phone at the domestic terminal to let him know that she had arrived in Auckland and that she loved him now more than ever. A romantic energy swirled around in her tummy for the entire flight to Christchurch.

A fit, young man about her age sat next to her on the plane and man-spread his legs into Jenae's seat space. As she crossed her legs to prevent them from touching his, she struck up a conversation with him.

"Are you going home or visiting in Christchurch?" Jenae asked the stranger.

"I'm going home to visit my mum and sister for Christmas. I'm from there, but I've been living in Australia for the last five years."

"What do you do in Australia?" Jenae asked.

"I'm a footballer in one of the professional leagues over there."

"Football as in soccer or rugby?"

"Soccer. Where did you come from? Your accent isn't from around here."

"I'm from America. Have you been there?" Jenae asked.

"No, not yet. I'm hoping to get there sometime soon. A lot of Kiwi's feel like we know about America because all of the movies are made there. You know Hollywood and all."

"I've never thought of it that way. Interesting perspective. Most of America is very different from blockbuster movies, although we do have real cowboys in Texas," Jenae said.

"It's so cool to see the big movies. They put millions of dollars into each film, and I get to watch them in a dark theater with a huge screen for a few bucks."

The flight attendant picked up the plastic cups and peanut packaging as the plane circled the airport and Jenae tightened her seatbelt in preparation for landing. She cranked her neck to look out the small window of the plane to see if she recognized any landmarks. She could only make out the large cathedral in the middle of downtown. The turquoise tip on the top of the bell tower gave it away. The landing was smooth among the pastures of green, and they were the only plane in sight, except for the gray U.S. military planes on the other side of the airport that were preparing for flights to Antarctica.

Jenae felt weirdly at home—like her seat mate who had been living abroad in Australia.

Neve waited against the wall closest to the gate where Jenae would appear. He thought about it as being a magic act that he had seen in Las Vegas. '*Abracadabra* . . . and she appeared out of a big tin can,' Neve thought. The reunion was sweet for Jenae when Neve slowly walked to meet her with a loving smile and a bouquet of flowers with her favorite freesias. Jenae was exhausted and fell into his arms for a long hug. They walked together to a more private area for a tender kiss. Neve slung her carry-on luggage over his shoulder and held her hand as they talked about the flight. Neve was jealous that he missed anytime in the air. They stopped at baggage claim to hug and kiss, like tasting a snack before the big meal.

In the parking lot, they started on the appetizer by kissing and heavy petting. Jenae felt satisfied before Neve did. He never wanted to stop, even if they stayed in the parking lot for hours. The parking fee was worth it.

"OK, we can go to my mum's now. It's just that we won't have any privacy while she's home."

"We can figure it out. I'm looking forward to seeing Helen again," Jenae said.

"I've planned a few fun days in Southland for us. I used to work there in my cop days, and I think you'll like the glaciers and beaches along the way," Neve said.

"Can we go to Queenstown? I heard there are some really fun activities there," Jenae asked.

"Of course. I was thinking we could leave tomorrow to make our way down there, stay for a few days, and come back here for the Christmas festivities."

"Are you going to go to Christmas church service with me?" Jenae asked.

"You know I'm not a churchy person. We occasionally went to Mass when I was young. My dad was Catholic, and when my parents split up, we stopped going altogether. Too many consequences," Neve said.

"I can see that, but I don't go very often, and this is the one time that means a lot to me. Think about it," Jenae responded.

Neve nodded and pointed out a raft of ducks swimming on a pond as he stopped at a red light.

<hr>

Helen was waiting for the couple when they arrived. She had made ham sandwiches with clarified butter and sweet gherkin pickles for lunch.

"Welcome back, Jenae!" Helen gave Jenae a big hug and sat her down at the kitchen table with a sandwich and a cup of tea.

"You don't take milk in your tea, do you?"

"No, just black for me please," Jenae said.

After catching up on school and work and the plane ride, Helen excused herself.

"I'm sorry, I have to run. I'm meeting my beau at the gym, and then we're going out for a drink afterward."

"You're looking really fit, Helen! Sounds like you might fancy this gentleman," Jenae said.

"I don't know if he's a gentleman, but he sure is fun!" Helen said.

"Oh, Mum. I don't want to hear that," Neve said.

"Well, I better get to it. You should probably rest this afternoon after that long flight," Helen said as she grabbed her duffle bag and keys.

"Bye, have a good workout. Thanks for tea!" Jenae smiled as Helen waved back at her.

Lunch gave Neve and Jenae the fuel to serve up the main course of lovemaking in the bedroom. Sex in the middle of the day was extra exciting, because the light streamed through the windows, and they could hear the neighbor mowing his lawn over the back fence. They could be as loud as they wanted; especially when the gardener made passes near the property line.

⸺◆⸺

The next day started bright and early, with a driving excursion to the Southland. They took the central route so they could spend the first night in Queenstown as Jenae requested. There weren't many places to stop, but they'd had a few unscheduled delays on the road while farmers moved their mobs of sheep from one field to the next further down the road.

"Do you think Bill will let me help with lambing like he promised?" Jenae asked.

"I think he's counting on your help. I told him we'd be back in five or six days," Neve said.

"Good, I can't wait. But I didn't get a chance to get boots for the occasion. I got really sick off a Portuguese donut on my last day of work. I was going to go shopping for this trip but couldn't get out of bed. I'll have to borrow Tee's again I suppose."

"How did you get sick on a donut?" Neve asked.

"I think there was a hefty dose of egg whites in the one I got. The box specifically indicated no egg, but maybe it got mixed up. I'm pretty sure it was an allergic reaction; I'm just glad it didn't stop me from making my flight. Thanks for buying my ticket by the way."

"Sure, it's the least I could do. I made a bunch of money on energy trades, and I feel horrible about breaking up with you over that wanker FBI guy. I know that you were trying to get my visa, I appreciate all that you went through."

"About that . . . you were 100% right about him. I want to sincerely apologize in person and tell you everything that Logan was up to. I left you the message about the basics, but thought I should wait to bring you up to speed until after your big exams. Plus, I couldn't afford a long phone call."

"What else do you need to tell me?" Neve took a double take as Jenae explained.

"Basically, Logan the FBI guy is a legitimate psychopathic stalker."

"What did he do to you?"

"Remember Angel Island where we went hiking one day? We took the ferry from Tiburon?"

"Yes, it was when I realized that I truly loved you. Riding on the ferry out on the water was romantic." Neve smiled.

"Don't get mad, but I went there with Logan. He said he had information about your visa process. He was bread-crumbing me along by promising to get your immigration status taken care of."

"Jesus, Jenae. That was so dangerous going to that deserted island with him."

"There were lots of people from the ferry, and we brought bikes, too."

"What happened? You told me that I was right about him, so I like that part of the story."

"Logan told me that he was the reason that you had to leave the country. He had friends that made it happen, and it would take a miracle to get you back in. I suppose he made false allegations against you, or something like that. Then, Logan confessed to sending that green-eyed bandit to scare me in Dallas, and he admitted to placing the dolphin and heart bracelet into my bag in Hawaii . . . and it did have a tracker in it."

"Are you kidding me? What a fucking asshole!"

"That's not all. He made the call with the suspicious tip that led to the SWAT at my Marina apartment. I don't know how anyone's mind could be so diabolical."

"I guess you're going to have to move here then if we get married." Neve blurted and wished he could capture all the words and swallow them again.

"Do you want to marry me?" Jenae teased. "You do want to marry me." She smiled.

Neve shook his head and looked out the window.

<hr>

Queenstown was buzzing with summer tourists, and the weather was perfect. They found a small hotel along the lake and made reservations at a restaurant on a mountaintop. Neve promised to bring her back for more activities later, because he wanted to make it all the way to Stewart Island for a few days. The southern-most point closest to Antarctica looked tropical in the summertime, with white sand beaches and turquoise blue waters. Neve had fond memories of finding stray penguins along the beaches in his earlier days on family vacations. What Jenae didn't know was that he had planned a fixed plane ride for the two of them, from Invercargill to the island. His buddy from aviation school was working that route as a pilot over the summer and offered Neve and Jenae a free flight. Neve saw it as an opportunity to get his foot in the door for building flight hours in the future, even if it was thirty minutes at a time.

"Are you ready for a few nights on a natural island? A beautiful Island for a beautiful gal."

"Is this tiny plane safe? You know my dad and mom had their private plane licenses. We took vacations in a tiny Cessna. Besides my dad scaring the crap out of me by flying weightless, my sister threw up a lot. In fact, I think during one weightless dive, little mandarin orange slices float in front of my face. They had emerged from her stomach."

"That's grotesque and cool at the same time. Maybe we should wait to have lunch when we get there," Neve said.

"Good idea," Jenae said.

"I want to go swimming in the clear blue waters and find jewel rocks on the beach. We might even see a Kiwi bird if we hike at night. They're sneaky little buggers. You know they are the country mascot, but Stewart Island is the best chance to see them. They say it's the original New Zealand."

The party of six landed on Stewart Island without incident, and Jenae and Neve headed to the local brewpub for a basket of fried blue cod and chips with a few pints. The fresh catch was more delicious than the fish and chips that she'd had last time after a night of bar hopping in Christchurch.

The week ended with a jet boat ride in Fiordland and hiking through the dense forest. Jenae didn't see penguins this time, but vowed to come back again. Glaciers, waterfalls, deep lakes, and strange little animals and birds mesmerized her. Thankfully, there were no snakes. Neve loved all kinds of animals, which gave Jenae hope that he would eventually desire children if they were ever to get married. But she recognized he had dreams and goals that he wanted to achieve before children settled him into a routine. She was willing to be patient—for a while.

Chapter 30

Birth Days

Bill collected on his promise to test Jenae's labor and delivery skills, except she would have to expand her knowledge to birthing in a barn. She borrowed the appropriate lambing gear from Tee and was the most enthusiastic midwife mentee Bill had ever trained. Neve dropped her off at the farm on his way to the airfield. He had some flight time scheduled and wanted to avoid the blood and guts extravaganza. Mama ewes had one, two, or three lambs per pregnancy, and the farmer had to be on high alert during lambing season to make sure the ewe delivered the lambs and placenta properly. Jenae was mostly there to help the babies latch on to nurse for the first few feedings and to make sure the new mamas had enough extra hay and feed to keep their milk supplies up.

One stubborn, and possibly traumatized ewe, dismissed her lamb and completely rejected it. Jenae made it her mission to find another mama of a singlet to take care of the orphaned lamb. She introduced the baby to three ewes before she found a surrogate. The new mama sniffed the baby and pulled it into her belly to nurse off the teat that hadn't been emptied by her own offspring. She seemed almost satisfied to have two babies instead of just one. She licked the dried afterbirth off of the lamb's face and legs and tummy, putting her scent on it to make it her own.

The fourteen-hour day and night was exhausting, but the satisfaction of helping to bring life into the world made Jenae grateful. She thought about the beauty of the land surrounding her and the opportunities to make huge leaps for love with Neve.

Since Jenae didn't have the chance to shop for Neve and his family before she left San Francisco, she convinced Neve to go downtown and find Christmas gifts for all of his family.

"You really don't have to get them anything," Neve said.

"Of course I do. I'm sure they have something for me to unwrap on Christmas Eve. Do you unwrap gifts on Christmas Eve or on Christmas morning?" Jenae asked.

"As kids, we would wake at the break of dawn and tear downstairs on Christmas morning. Now that we're all adults, we open after Christmas tea in the afternoon or early evening."

"Oh God, are we supposed to cook something for the feast? Shrimp on the barbie or something like that since it's hot out and its summertime?"

"Not a chance. That's the Aussies. We do the traditional English Christmas dinner with ham, and turkey, and blood pudding and ambrosia salad."

"Don't forget the fruitcake!" Jenae added.

"YUM," Neve teased her.

After shopping for gifts, they bought groceries to prepare glazed carrots and mashed potatoes—Jenae's favorites. Neve picked up a few pomegranates to mix with champagne that he'd gotten from the liquor store. He was planning on a big celebration, and Christmas Eve was a night spent at the pub with friends and family. It was a night to reflect on blessings and challenges throughout the year.

Jenae thought back on the major events in her life. It started with Neve moving her from Dallas to San Francisco. She started at a new school for her MBA; she traveled to New Zealand for the first time and now a second time. She was stalked by a madman and had no idea if he was still a threat to her, and she lived through the one of the biggest earthquakes in U.S. history. And she fell in love with a man on the other side of the world. Her knees buckled a bit when she thought about it. She wasn't sure what would come next, but she had a compelling urge to thank Jesus for getting her through it. It was his birthday after all.

"Hey, what time is it?" Jenae asked Neve as the pub crowd dissipated.

He looked at his worn-out wristwatch, and Jenae thought about how much he was going to love the new aviator watch that she had just wrapped for him to open after Christmas dinner.

"Ah, it looks like it's coming up on 11:45," Neve replied.

"We should probably go to midnight services at the Cathedral; it's going to be at least a fifteen-minute walk from here," Jenae said.

"Do we have to go? We're having such a good time. Why do you want to ruin it by going to church? It's so boring," Neve slurred over the foam on his beer.

"What do you mean boring? It's Christmas Eve and its church, what do you expect?" Jenae said.

"I just want to stay here at the pub with you and my friends and my siblings. You're going to have to learn to do things my way, Jenae. Hey, I just rhymed. I'm a poet, and I didn't know it." Neve laughed at his drunken joke, and Jenae had enough. She fumed out of the pub, and into the fairy lit streets leading to the cathedral. She would've been angrier had Neve been sober, but she knew he'd been working on his traumas with a therapist and had made a lot of progress. *He's just stupid and blowing off some steam tonight,* Jenae thought to herself as she breathed in the warm summer night air. She was perfectly comfortable going to church by herself. She liked the solitude of prayer, but also loved the beauty of the church and power of communal prayer.

Meanwhile, back at the pub, Neve's siblings and friends berated him for letting her go by herself. They had to remind him he had a ring in his pocket, and they were all there to witness a proposal.

"Ah, bloody hell. I fucked it up. I drank too many pints. I was just having so much fun," Neve slurred.

"Well, you're officially an idiot, Neve," Tee said.

"Come on, let's get you sober. How much time do we have before Mass is over, an hour at least right?" Hamish asked.

They took his beer away and replaced it with two cups of water. And then gave him a handful of pretzels and peanuts and another two cups of water.

"Come on Romeo, we're going to walk this off."

"Hold on. Let me hit the loo first," Neve responded.

After emptying his bladder, he stopped to look in the mirror while he washed his hands.

"You can do this Neve," he said to his reflection. "She's the one." He splashed his face with cold water and ran his wet fingers through his hair.

When he walked outside, his entourage was waiting to escort him to the cathedral for the remainder of midnight Mass. Neve patted his front pocket that held the decent sized, close to perfect diamond ring that had excellent color and clarity. He had made several visits to the jeweler to pick out the right one on a tight budget.

The cathedral looked different at night, and Christmas decorations made it stand out as the most beautiful building in the whole city. Neve left his friends behind at the town square and entered the church by himself. He was anxious at first, but a sense of calm overcame him when he saw Jenae silently praying in a pew not too far from the back. He wondered what she was praying for. *Did she give thanks for their relationship? Was she mad and praying for a way out? Maybe she was praying for clarity—for a sign.*

After the last prayer and blessing from the priest, Neve slipped out of the church before the procession started down the main aisle. He walked to the other side of the town square away from the church to wait for Jenae to exit. He wanted space and privacy for his proposal to either be accepted or declined.

After watching almost every parishioner walk away from the church, Jenae finally appeared. She walked in Neve's direction without seeing him in the shadows.

He didn't say a word as he walked slowly toward her, admiring her glowing smile.

"You missed Mass!" she said when he waved at her.

"I saw a little bit of it. I saw you praying and got a blessing before I left. That's a whole lot for me."

"You should have sat with me."

"Next time I will."

"Next Christmas?" Jenae asked.

"Next anytime, I will be by your side in that pew."

Jenae's heart swelled.

"In fact, I will be beside you for the rest of your life, if you'll allow it."

Neve carefully kneeled on the cobblestone square and held Jenae's hand as he pulled out the ring box.

"Jenae, you are the love of my life, and we have been through a lot. I hope you are willing to continue our journey together. Jenae, will you give me the honor of being my wife? I so desperately want to be your husband and be by your side. I love you, Jenae. Will you marry me?"

Neve opened the box and stood up to take out the solitary diamond engagement ring to show it to her.

"YES! I will marry you, Neve. I love you so much."

The entourage watching from the sidewalk cheered when they heard Jenae's answer.

The next night, the Christmas family feast had a special meaning as Jenae showed off her nearly perfect, decent sized diamond ring. She was elated to know that she belonged to someone she loved and craved.

After dinner, Helen turned on the TV to look for Christmas movies, and Neve and Jenae snuggled near the yellow and orange glow from the fireplace.

"What do you want to watch? Christmas Mass?" Helen asked.

"Ha, ha. I think Neve had his limit," Jenae said.

"Does anyone want anything from the kitchen? I'm going to get a snack. I think I saw some leftover Christmas cake," Neve asked.

Helen paused on a Sky News reporter who warned about increased suicides during the holiday season. He was reporting live from a place Jenae knew well; The Golden Gate Bridge in San Francisco, California.

Jenae stood up to get closer to the TV for a better look. The reporter explained the city had seen an increase in jumpers; most likely due to trauma from the recent earthquake coupled with loneliness of the holidays.

The reporter described a pair of shiny, businessman shoes that were neatly left behind on the bridge with a wallet placed inside. "The presumed jumper was one of the nation's finest FBI agents. The name of the owner of the shoes would be withheld until his death was verified and after the next of kin was notified."

"Neve, come listen . . . quick!"

"What's going on?" Neve said as he placed a plate of sliced Christmas cake slathered with butter on the coffee table.

Jenae's face turned pale white, and her legs buckled when she reached back and sat down on the nearest chair. She gasped as she pointed to the picture on the TV screen of a pair of men's Florsheim shoes with red aglet tips on the shoe laces.

"I've seen those shoes before! Logan wore those shoes," Jenae said.

Jenae and Neve looked at each other with slack jaws. "Could it be? Logan?" Neve said.

Jenae's stomach dropped. She felt relieved. At the same time she felt guilt for being relieved.

"If it was him, my prayers for peace tonight technically would be answered. But I didn't see that coming," Jenae said.

"You may think it's an answer for peace, but I wouldn't count on Logan's demise. He's a psychopath and I won't believe that he's dead until I see evidence of his lifeless body. I feel guilty for not feeling sadness, but I'm not convinced."

I have to believe he's gone. Maybe justice has been served. I'm afraid to see what would happen if I go back to America if he is still out there. For sure, those are his shoes. He has to be dead. Jenae thought.

Neve comforted Jenae. "Maybe it is a Christmas Blessing." Neve guiltily breathed a sigh of relief and looked upward, while Jenae hugged him from behind with her new ring glistening in the fire's glow.

THE END

Also by Reggie Brick

BIG ROCK – Passion in the Pacific
BIG KIWI – Suspense Under Southern Skies

Connect with Reggie:
https://linktr.ee/reggiebrick

Big Bay Characters

J enae – Nurse and MBA student who recently finished a three month traveling nurse assignment in Hawaii (Big Rock). She is serious about her career and about love

IT – Big Strong co-worker and friend to Jenae.

Neve (AKA Neville) – A handsome love interest of Jenae's from New Zealand

Deely – U.S. Air Force pilot friend of Neve's

Logan – Obsessed FBI agent

Kyle – MBA friend from Dallas

Kristine – Nurse friend and former roommate from Dallas

Boston Johnny – A courter of Jenae

Hamish – Neve's brother

Sandy – Good friend and confident who dated Jenae's brother

Pami – Long time nurse friend from San Antonio and Hawaii

Annie – Jenae's roommate in the Marina District

Paulina – Jenae's second roommate

Joe – Upstairs neighbor

<u>Zeki</u> – Turkish MBA classmate

<u>Helen</u> – Neve's mother

<u>Peter</u> – Neve's father

<u>Tee</u> – Neve's younger sister

<u>Bill</u> – Tee's serious boyfriend and farmer